THROUGH THICK AND THIN

The next moment they were fighting fiercely, furiously

FRANK RICHARDS

THROUGH THICK AND THIN

SPRING BOOKS · LONDON

Published by

SPRING BOOKS

SPRING HOUSE · SPRING PLACE · LONDON NW 5

Printed in Czechoslovakia

CONTENTS

LIST OF ILLUSTRATIONS

CHAPTER I

D'ARCY IN THE DARK

'WALK it!' said Talbot.

He jumped off his bicycle.

'I suppose we had bettah!' sighed Arthur Augustus D'Arcy.

'Much better.'

'Wotten!' said Arthur Augustus.

And he, too, dismounted.

He stood in the darkness of Wayland Lane, holding his machine, with an expression of dismay on his aristocratic face.

There was not a glimmer of light on his machine.

Talbot's lamp was brightly gleaming. Talbot of the Shell was not the fellow to omit affixing his lamp before he started on a long spin on a winter's afternoon. D'Arcy of the Fourth was exactly the fellow to forget to do so: and he had duly forgotten.

Certainly Arthur Augustus had expected to be back at St. Jim's well before dark: so had Talbot.

But while Talbot was prepared for possible eventualities, Arthur Augustus was not.

They had gone for a spin after class. It was wintry weather, fine but cold, with a feeling of frost in the air: just the weather, in fact, for an enjoyable spin. But a puncture several miles from home was less enjoyable. Arthur Augustus had not thought anything about possible punctures. In fact, he hadn't packed his puncture outfit.

Luckily, Talbot had.

That puncture had caused delay — considerable delay. When they resumed the ride, the shades of night were falling fast, as the poet has expressed it.

They were going to be late for lock-ups at the school. That did not worry them unduly: for they had no doubt that their house-master, Mr. Railton, would take a mild view, making due allowance for that unlucky puncture. All would have been well, or almost well, if there had been a lamp on Gussy's bike.

But Gussy's bike-lamp was reposing in the bike-shed at St. Jim's.

Had his pals in the Fourth, Blake and Herries and Digby, been with him, they would certainly have told him, in emphatic terms, what they thought of a fellow who forgot to put a lamp on his jigger.

Luckily, it was Talbot of the Shell who was with

him: and Talbot of the Shell was a fellow of infinite patience and good temper.

It was past lighting-up time. Under the branches in Wayland Lane it was almost as black as a hat. Arthur Augustus was, perhaps, tempted to take a chance. Talbot settled that point by dismounting.

'Wotten!' repeated Arthur Augustus, dismally. 'We're still miles from the school, Talbot, deah boy.'

'About a mile and a half,' said Talbot. 'Can't be helped, old chap! Can't ride without a light after dark.'

'It will mean lines.'

'Well, we've had lines before, and lived to tell the tale,' said Talbot, with a smile. 'Push on, Gussy.'

'We shall be fwightfully late, walkin' it.'

'Later still if we stand here chatting, old chap! You're good for a mile and a half on Shanks's pony.'

'Yaas, wathah! But —' Arthur Augustus paused, and he did not push his bike.

'We're wasting time,' hinted Talbot: a much milder remark than Blake or Herries or Digby would have made, in the circumstances.

Arthur Augustus shook his head.

'I shall be fwightfully late, and I expect I shall get into a wow!' he said. 'No need for you to get into a wow too, Talbot. You had bettah cut on, and leave me to walk it.'

'I'm sticking to you.'

'I weally wish I had wemembahed to stick on my lamp!' sighed Arthur Augustus. 'Howevah, it is too late to think of that now.'

'Somewhat!' agreed Talbot. 'Come on, D'Arcy, and put your best foot foremost. We'll walk it together.'

Arthur Augustus D'Arcy shook his noble head again.

'Not at all, deah boy,' he answered. 'I cannot allow you to get into a wow for nothin'. You wide on —'

'I'd rather stick to you, really.'

'Wubbish!' said Arthur Augustus, decidedly. 'It is weally all my fault, for forgettin' to stick on my lamp. Wide on, and get in as soon as you can, and leave me to walk it.'

'But —!' said Talbot.

'I insist, deah boy!' said Arthur Augustus, firmly.

Talbot of the Shell hesitated.

'A wow for one is bettah than a wow for two!' said Arthur Augustus. 'I insist upon your widin' on, Talbot.'

'Oh, all right, then!' said Talbot, at last.

He put a leg over his machine.

'That's wight, deah boy,' said Arthur Augustus, 'push on as fast as you can, and you won't be vewy late. Wide like anythin'.'

'Okay,' said Talbot.

And he pushed at his pedals and rode on, leaving the swell of St. Jim's to walk it. He did not like leaving Arthur Augustus on his own: but really Gussy was right: a row for one was better than a row for two. He disappeared into the darkness, the gleam of his rear-light vanishing round a winding of the lane.

'Wotten!' repeated Arthur Augustus, dismally.

He wheeled on his bike.

He had a mile and a half to walk, pushing his jigger, and an interview with his house-master to follow, when he arrived at long last at St. Jim's. It was not a pleasant prospect.

He paused again.

'I wondah —!' he murmured.

Like so many fellows in such a jam, Arthur Augustus was considering whether, just for once, he might take a chance, and ride without a light after lighting-up time. It was an infraction of the law: it was a reckless act: it might cause an accident. But—!

Arthur Augustus was quite a law-abiding person. He was not by any means reckless or inconsiderate. But —

'Just this once!' murmured Gussy.

He looked round him. The darkness was dense. Undoubtedly any vehicle on that shadowy lane needed a light. But —!

It was a lonely lane. Really, nobody was likely to get in the way. The lane at that point skirted the park wall of Wayland Grange, over-topped by dim trees. Could he chance it — just for once?

Sad to relate, Arthur Augustus, like so many cyclists similarly situated, fell to the temptation. He was going to be very careful; very watchful and wary: he was not going to run into any pedestrian who might chance to come along: in fact, he thought of all the reasons for doing what, at the back of his mind, he knew he ought not to do. He remounted his machine and rode!

He was, indeed, very careful. He kept quite near the park wall, leaving the road clear for any traffic that might materialise. And he was taken utterly by surprise when, all of a sudden, a shadowy figure dropped from the park wall in front of him.

He hardly saw it, before he crashed.

Arthur Augustus had thought of everything else. He had thought of possible pedestrians: of vehicles behind and before: but naturally enough, it had never occurred to him that some person inside the walls of Wayland Grange might climb the park

All of a sudden, a shadowy figure dropped from the park wall in front of him

wall from inside and drop into the road. Really, no fellow could have foreseen such an occurrence.

Unluckily, that was what occurred.

D'Arcy, and his bike, were invisible in the darkness. The person who dropped from the wall had not the remotest idea that a cyclist was coming along in the dark. He knew — the next moment!

'Bai Jove!'

'Oh!'

Crash!

An unseen figure went over, yelling. Arthur Augustus's bike went over that figure, clanking. Arthur Augustus, pitched headlong from the saddle, went over the bike, sprawling and gasping. It was quite a mix-up under the shadowy branches that over-topped the wall of Wayland Grange.

CHAPTER II

UNEXPECTED

'OH!' exclaimed Talbot.

He jammed on his brake.

'That ass!' he breathed.

Across the dark fields came sounds of alarm. It was only a matter of minutes since he had left Arthur Augustus D'Arcy to 'walk it', though the winding of the country lane, and the high hedges, had hidden his lights from the swell of St. Jim's. A field separated him from the spot where he had left Arthur Augustus: and across that field, startling sounds reached his ears. A couple of minutes more, and he would have been out of hearing. As it was, he heard the uproar very distinctly.

There had been a crash and a clanging, and two voices raised on their top notes. One of them was still raised: and though Talbot could not distinguish the words, he knew D'Arcy's voice.

Evidently the swell of the Fourth had struck trouble.

'That ass!' repeated Talbot.

He whirled round his bicycle and rode back. Something, evidently, had happened to D'Arcy in the dark. Nothing was likely to have happened to him had he been wheeling his unlighted bike: and Talbot could guess that, after he had left him, Gussy had yielded to the temptation to ride without a light. Apparently he had run into somebody — not a surprising happening on an unlighted bike after dark.

Talbot drove hard at the pedals, and his machine fairly flew, his lamp gleaming ahead. He came back round the bend of the winding lane as if riding in a race.

'Oh!' he exclaimed, as his light picked up the figures by the park wall, under the over-topping branches.

A bike lay curled up in the road. Arthur Augustus was standing with his back to the park wall, his eyeglass streaming at the end of its cord, his hands up and his face wildly excited. He was defending himself, as well as he could, against a slogging attack. A man, small in stature, dressed in dark clothes, was punching at him savagely. Small as the man was, he was evidently more than a match for the Fourth-former of St. Jim's: and Arthur Augustus was collecting a rapid series of hefty punches.

'Keep off, you wottah!' came a yell from Arthur

Augustus. 'You fwightful wuffian, stoppit! Oh,
cwikey! Oh, cwumbs! You uttah wuffian — ow!
wow!'

'Take that —' came a savage, growling voice.
'Oh cwikey!'

'And that — and that. And that — you clumsy
young fool! And that — and that — and that —
knocking a man over in the dark, you mad young
idiot — take that — and that — and that — and
that —'

'Yawooooooooooh!'

Arthur Augustus was taking them: he had no
choice about that. The little man in dark clothes
was hitting hard, and hitting often.

Evidently he had been knocked over by the
cyclist riding an unlighted bike. No doubt he had
been hurt. That was more than enough to make
even a good-tempered man angry: and it was not,
perhaps, surprising that he felt an urge to punch
the cyclist who had downed him. But that savage
attack was altogether beyond the limit. Had there
been no help at hand for Arthur Augustus, he
would undoubtedly have been severely damaged.

But there was help at hand.

Talbot of the Shell came on the scene almost like
lightning. He leaped from his bike, leaving it to
whirl away, and rushed to the rescue. Before either

of the combatants knew he was there, he had grasped the little man by the back of the collar and dragged him backwards by main force.

So powerful was that wrench that the little man went spinning, and crashed headlong in the road when Talbot released his collar.

'Gussy, old man —!' panted Talbot.

'Oh, cwikey! Oh, cwumbs!' gasped Arthur Augustus, dizzily. 'Is that you, Talbot, old chap?'

'Yes, yes! I heard you, across the fields, and came back! Has that brute hurt you, old fellow?'

'Yaas, wathah!' Arthur Augustus rubbed his eye with one hand, his noble nose with the other. 'Oh cwikey! The wotten wuffian pitched into me like a wildcat — weally like a wegular wildcat! Oh cwumbs!'

'He won't touch you again,' said Talbot, setting his lips.

The little man was sitting up in the road, panting. Talbot turned to him, with a grim brow. The slim swell of the Fourth was no match for his assailant: but Talbot of the Shell certainly was. He was prepared to give the savage-tempered fellow all that he asked for, and a little over.

'Thank goodness you heard, and came back, old chap!' gasped Arthur Augustus. 'He was wathah too much for me! The fwightful wuffian —'

'You ran into him — ?'

'Yaas, and I am quite awah, Talbot, that I should not have been widin' without a light: but how was I to know that anybody was goin' to dwop ovah that wall —'

'Over that wall?' repeated Talbot.

'Yaas, wathah! He dwopped just in fwont of my jiggah, and it weally could not be helped. Why couldn't the silly ass come out at the gate, if he wanted to come out? Dwoppin' ovah a wall suddenly in the dark —'

'He can't have been up to any good there, if that was the way he was coming out,' said Talbot. 'People who belong to Wayland Grange don't get out over the park wall.'

'Look out, deah boy!' exclaimed Arthur Augustus, suddenly. The man in the road had scrambled up. He came back towards the two schoolboys with fists clenched and eyes glittering.

Talbot faced him coolly.

'Stand back!' he rapped.

'Get out of the way,' came a savage growl. 'I've been knocked over by that mad young fool, riding without a light, and I'm going to smash him.'

'You've done more than enough in that line,' said Talbot quietly. 'If you want any more, you'll tackle me.'

'I'll do that fast enough if you don't get out of the way.'

'Just as you like!'

The man came on with a rush. But he found the strong, sturdy Shell fellow a very different proposition from the slim swell of the Fourth. Talbot's hands were up, his eyes gleaming over them.

He knocked aside a savage jab, and hit out, with all the strength of a strong right arm. The angry man was bowled over like a skittle. He went back into the road — on his back — with a yell.

'Bai Jove!' ejaculated Arthur Augustus, 'man down, deah boy! I must wemark, Talbot, that you pack a wathah good punch!'

Talbot did not reply: his eyes were watchfully on the man in the road. The fellow scrambled up again: but he did not make another rush. That one drive seemed to be all that he wanted.

He stood rubbing his chin, eyeing the two schoolboys evilly in the dim shadows. Then he bent and rubbed his knee. Apparently his knee had suffered in the collision. Talbot's bike had curled up by the roadside, the light gleaming from the ground on the scene.

As the little man bent to rub his knee, that gleam shone on his face. It revealed a hard set of features, a mouth like a vice, and two eyes that glittered like a rat's. Hitherto, his face had been merely a dim shadow: now they saw it clear and plain: and Talbot, as he saw it, gave a violent start.

'Smug!' he ejaculated.

The strange name dropped from his lips involuntarily. The colour in his own face faded, as he stared at the hard, foxy features.

The little man straightened up, startled.

'What's that?' he snarled. 'What you calling me? Who are you? How d'you know —? Who are you?'

Talbot did not answer. The man's face was dim again now, but the Shell fellow of St. Jim's stood staring at it.

The man groped in a pocket. The next moment an electric torch gleamed out, the light full on Talbot's face.

Then there was an exclamation from the man whom Talbot called by the strange name of 'Smug'.

'The Toff!'

Arthur Augustus D'Arcy looked on in wonder.

'Toff!' repeated the little man with the foxy face. 'Gum! If I'd known it was you, Toff, I wouldn't have cut up rusty. Birds of a feather, what, Toff?'

He chuckled.

'Get out!' Talbot's voice was husky. He came

towards the man, his fists clenched hard. 'Get out
of this!'

'Look here, Toff —'

'Get out of it, I say, or I'll beat you till you can't
crawl away on your hands and knees.' Talbot's
voice rose, 'Get out, you rat.'

'I tell you — hands off!' yelled Smug, as the
Shell fellow came at him. 'Strike me pink — hands
off, Toff!'

He backed away, turned and ran. Talbot made
a stride after him — but he turned back, as the
running man vanished in the darkness.

'Talbot, deah boy —!' gasped Arthur Augustus.

'Let's get going,' said Talbot, abruptly.

'But weally, Talbot —'

'For goodness' sake, get going — don't you
want to get back to the school before the milk in
the morning!' exclaimed Talbot, roughly.

'Weally, Talbot —'

'Get going, fathead!'

Arthur Augustus made no reply, but he compressed his noble lips. He gave his nose a final rub
and picked up his machine.

'Pway wide on, Talbot,' he said stiffly. 'I am
vewy much obliged to you for comin' back to my
help, but you can wide on now —'

'Oh, rats!'

Talbot picked up his bicycle, and wheeled it.
Arthur Augustus followed on, pushing his jigger.
After what had happened, the swell of St. Jim's
was not feeling disposed to 'chance it' again, riding
without a light. They pushed on round the corner
of the lane.

'Talbot —!' recommenced Arthur Augustus.

'Oh, don't chatter.'

'Bai Jove!'

Arthur Augustus, really, could hardly believe
his aristocratic ears. Never before had he heard
anything like that from Talbot of the Shell. Talbot
was always quiet and civil: a little reserved, perhaps, but always kind and patient and of unfailing
good temper. He seemed strangely changed now.
Arthur Augustus breathed very hard.

'I will not inflict my conversation on you, Talbot, if you do not desiah to hear me,' he said with
tremendous dignity. 'I was only goin' to wemark—'

'For goodness' sake be quiet.'

'I was goin' to wemark —'

'Pack it up!'

'To wemark that I should pwefer you to wide
on, and leave me to walk my jiggah on my own.'

Talbot gave him a look, with knitted brows.
Then, without answering, he put a leg over his
machine and rode.

'Bai Jove!' murmured Arthur Augustus. 'Talbot's mannahs seem to be detewiowatin' vewy much — vewy much indeed. I am quite surpwised at him.'

Arthur Augustus shook his noble head; and stepped out wearily on his long tramp to St. Jim's.

CHAPTER III

LOOKING AFTER LOWTHER

'HA, ha, ha!'

It was Monty Lowther who gave utterance to that trill of merriment, in No. 10 study in the Shell.

Tom Merry and Manners looked round at him.

Lowther had just come into the study. He came in with a grin on his face. Something, evidently, amused Lowther. And he burst into a laugh as soon as he was in the study.

Tom Merry was sorting out books for preparation. Manners was packing films into a cardboard carton. Both those operations were suspended, as they cast inquiring looks at Monty.

'Well?' said Tom.

'Anything happened?' asked Manners.

'Not yet,' grinned Monty Lowther, 'but something's going to. No end of a jest on old Railton. Ha, ha, ha!'

At which both Monty's chums looked grave.

Monty was the funny man of the Shell. His

sense of humour was not always under restraint.
Anything in the nature of a jape had an irresistible
attraction for him. Often that propensity landed
him in a spot of bother. A 'jest' on Railton seemed
likely, to his chums, to land him in a larger spot
than usual. House-masters were not a proper subject
for jesting. Railton was a kind and good-tempered
man: but it was quite certain that he had no use
for jests from the funny man of the Shell.

'Fathead!' said Manners, tersely.

'Forget it!' said Tom Merry. 'You can't help
being a funny ass, Monty, but steer clear of house-
beaks. Jests on Railton are a bit more dangerous
than putting ink in D'Arcy's topper, or gum in
skimpole's cap. Just forget all about it.'

'You haven't heard what it is yet,' said Monty.

'Well, what is it, ass?'

Monty Lowther dived his hand into a pocket,
and held up a little, bright steel key. Manners and
Tom Merry gazed at it.

'That's Railton's,' said Monty.

'How on earth did you get hold of it, fathead?'

'Easy! It's the key of the money-drawer in his
desk in his study — lots of fellows have seen him
using it. I knew at once what it was when I spotted
it lying on the stairs. Railton must have dropped
it—slipped through a hole in the lining of a pocket,

perhaps — anyhow, there it was! Did I pounce on it at once?' Lowther chuckled.

'Why didn't you take it to him at once?' exclaimed Tom. 'Railton will be worried when he misses it.'

'He won't miss it for long,' said Lowther. 'He's going to find it sticking in the drawer where it belongs. I shall get a chance of nipping into his study when he goes along to Common-Room.'

'Oh, my hat!' said Manners. 'Is that what you call a jest on Railton?'

'That isn't all,' said Lowther. 'I can unlock the drawer with that key, see? Everybody knows that Railton keeps a lot of money in that drawer, for the House accounts and all sorts of things. Trimble saw it open once, and he says he saw a roll of bank-notes, and lots of currency notes, and —'

'You howling ass!' exclaimed Tom Merry, in alarm. 'Are you fathead enough to think of larking with money?'

'Oh, don't be such a solemn old judge!' exclaimed Lowther. 'I tell you it's a jest on Railton. He goes back to his study, and sees this key sticking in the money-drawer! That will make him jump, what?'

'Fathead!'

'Then he looks into the drawer to see that all's

safe — and finds that there's no money in it —'

'What?'

'Will he jump?' chuckled Lowther. 'A hundred pounds or so — missing! Gone from his gaze like a beautiful dream! Ha, ha, ha!'

Monty Lowther laughed again. His chums did not laugh. They gazed at him, speechless.

'Of course, the money won't be far away,' continued Lowther. 'Railton will find it — if he looks long enough — parked under the cushion on the seat of his arm-chair! Fancy his face! Ha, ha, ha!'

Again Monty Lowther had his laugh all to himself. Tom Merry and Manners did not look in the least amused. They looked horrified.

'You dithering ass!' gasped Tom, at last.

'You dangerous maniac!' hooted Manners.

'Oh draw it mild!' exclaimed Lowther, indignantly. 'No harm in a jest on old Railton, I suppose! You fellows haven't any sense of humour.'

'Not that sort, certainly,' said Tom. 'You unlimited chump, you're not going to lark with banknotes and currency notes. You're going to take that key back to Railton at once.'

'I'll watch it,' said Lowther.

'This minute!' exclaimed Manners.

'Oh, pack it up!' exclaimed Lowther, impatiently.

'I've told you what I'm going to do! I thought you'd laugh when I told you —'

'We'll laugh, if you like, after you've taken that key back to Railton,' said Tom. 'Have a little sense, old chap! Just a spot of commom sense! A fellow who handles other people's money might be suspected of pinching it.'

'I tell you Railton will find it in his arm-chair—'

'And suppose you were caught in the study, while you were handling it?' asked Manners.

'Rot!' said Lowther.

'For goodness' sake,' said Tom, 'take that key to Railton, or give it to me to take to him.'

'Rats!' said Lowther. 'Precious pair of wet blankets you fellows are.'

He turned to the door with a frown on his face, instead of a grin. Evidently, Monty had expected his chums to be amused by that jest on Railton! Their reception of his bright idea was disconcerting and exasperating, to a born japer.

'Hold on!' exclaimed Tom.

'Rats!' repeated Lowther.

But he had to hold on, as Tom Merry ran across the study, grasped him by the shoulder, and jerked him back from the door. Manners immediately placed himself between Monty and the doorway.

Lowther glared from one to the other.

'Look here,' he bawled, 'do you fancy you're going to stop me?'

'Just that!' said Tom. 'You're not going to play the mad ass, while you've got pals to look after you, old chap. Give me the key.'

'Go and eat coke!'

'Hand it over to Tom,' said Manners.

'Rats!'

'Then as jolly old Shakespeare says, we must be cruel only to be kind!' said Tom Merry. 'Bag him, Manners, old man.'

'What-ho!' said Manners, promptly.

'Look here — hands off — stoppit — oh crumbs!' gasped Lowther, as his faithful and loyal chums grasped him, hooked him off his feet, and sat him on the floor of No. 10 study. 'Leggo — wow! Chuck it — I'll jolly well — wooooh!'

The key clinked on the floor, as Monty Lowther struggled in the grasp of two pairs of hands. Tom Merry picked it up.

'Gimme that key!' yelled Lowther.

'Sit on him, Manners, while I take it down to Railton,' said Tom.

'Leave it to me,' grinned Manners.

Manners sat on his chum's chest, pinning him down. On his feet, no doubt Monty was a match for Harry Manners; but on his back, on the carpet with Manners sitting on his chest, he had no chance. He wriggled and struggled, and uttered dire threats of reprisals: but Manners sat tight and kept him pinned down, while Tom Merry walked out of the study with the key in his hand.

Tom lost no time. About a minute later he was tapping at the door of his house-master's study on the ground floor of the School House.

'Come in!' said Mr. Railton's deep voice.

Tom opened the door.

Mr. Railton was seated at his desk, deep in a Greek paper for the Sixth Form. He glanced up at Tom. Apparently he had not yet missed that key.

'What is it, Merry?' he asked.

Tom held up the key.

'I think this is yours, sir!' he said.

The house-master glanced at it, started and felt in his pocket. Tom laid it on the table.

'Bless my soul!' exclaimed the house-master. 'There is a hole in my pocket — I must have dropped the key!'

'Lowther found it on the stairs, sir!' said Tom. 'I thought I'd better bring it here at once.'

'Thank you very much,' said Mr. Railton, picking up the key. 'Please tell Lowther that I am very much obliged to him, Merry, for finding it.'

'Certainly, sir.'

Tom Merry left the house-master's study. As he closed the door and turned away, he almost ran into a Shell fellow coming up the passage.

'Oh Talbot!' he exclaimed. 'You're late in, old man.'

'That ass D'Arcy had a puncture,' said Talbot. 'I shall have to report to Railton. Bother the silly ass!'

He almost pushed past Tom Merry, to the house-master's door.

Tom gave him a rather curious look. Talbot's manner was short and sharp, almost surly: quite unlike his usual self. That Arthur Augustus D'Arcy was an ass, all his friends agreed: still, it was not like Talbot to speak as he had done.

Talbot tapped at the door and went in to see Mr. Railton. Tom headed for the staircase wondering a little what was up with Talbot. He came back into No. 10 study in the Shell, to find Manners still sitting on Monty Lowther, and Lowther breathing wrath.

'Okay, Manners,' said Tom. 'You can let him rip now.'

Manners removed himself from Lowther's chest.

Monty Lowther scrambled to his feet: red and breathless, and more than a little dusty. The look he gave his chums rivalled that of the fabled basilisk.

'You cheeky fatheads!' he bawled.

Tom Merry laughed.

'Go it!' he said. 'I've taken Railton's key back to him, so that's all right. Now slang us as much as you like, if it makes you feel better.'

'Yes, carry on, old fellow,' said Manners. 'Let off steam!'

'You silly, meddling, fatheaded, blithering, cheeky pair of dithering swobs!' roared Lowther.

'Hear, hear!' said Tom.

'Encore!' said Manners.

'I've a jolly good mind to punch your silly noses!' howled Lowther. 'You fatheaded, footling, cheeky ticks! Rats to both of you!'

Monty Lowther stamped out of the study, and closed the door after him with a terrific bang, that woke every echo in the Shell passage. They were great chums in No. 10 in the Shell: but Monty's look, as he departed, could not have been more unchummy. He stalked away down the passage in high wrath: leaving his faithful friends in No. 10 laughing!

CHAPTER IV

WHERE IS GUSSY?

'THAT ass!' said Jack Blake.

'That fathead!' said Herries.

'That chump!' said Digby.

Three Fourth-form fellows, in Study No. 6 in the Fourth, were sorting out their books for prep. Their remarks referred to the fourth member of that celebrated study, now conspicuous by his absence.

'Late for lock-ups!' said Blake. 'That means lines! And the silly ass looks like being late for prep too!'

'Railton will comb his hair if he's late for prep!' said Digby.

'Why the dickens hasn't he come in!' exclaimed Blake. 'If he'd gone out on his own he might have wandered anywhere — if there was a chance of losing the way Gussy's not the man to miss it! But he went for a spin with old Talbot, after class, and Talbot knows his way about. Talbot's come in —

35

Levison says he saw him going to Railton's study.
Where the dickens is Gussy?'

'Goodness knows!'

'I'll cut along and ask Talbot,' said Blake. 'He
must know, I suppose, as Gussy was with him.'

Blake left Study No. 6 and proceeded to the
Shell studies. He pitched open the door of No. 9
in the Shell, and looked in.

'Talbot —!' he began.

Gore and Skimpole were at the study table. Both
of them looked round at Jack Blake. But Talbot
was not to be seen.

'Isn't Talbot here?' rapped Blake.

'Can't you see he isn't?' rapped back Gore.

'Bother him!' grunted Blake.

He banged the door, and went on to No. 10.
Three juniors of the Shell were in that study: Tom
Merry and Manners and Lowther.

Lowther's voice was audible as Blake opened
the door.

'You silly asses, spoiling a jolly good jape —'
It was some little time since Monty Lowther had
been sat upon in that study: but he did not seem
to have quite recovered yet.

'You fellows know where Talbot is?' asked Blake.

'In his study, I expect,' said Tom Merry. 'It's
just on prep.'

'I've looked in, and he's not there. I want to ask him what's become of Gussy, as they were out together, and Gussy hasn't come in. Levison says that he's seen Talbot —'

'He's come in,' said Tom. 'I spoke to him going into Railton's study some time back. He said that D'Arcy had had a puncture —'

'He would!' said Blake, with a nod. 'If he couldn't lose his way, or run into a car, or skid into a ditch, he would have a puncture. Still, I suppose Talbot wouldn't leave him to enjoy his puncture all on his own. He would lend him a hand mending it.'

'Sure to,' said Tom.

'Bother both of 'em!' said Blake, and he shut the door of No. 10 and went back down the passage.

Most of the School House juniors were now in their studies, or coming up to prep. Blake glanced over a dozen or more on the landing and the stairs, but failed to see Talbot among them.

'Seen Talbot, Cardew?' he called out.

Cardew laughed.

'Yes! If you want to see a bear with a sore head go down to the day-room, and you'll see him there.'

Blake stared.

'What the dickens do you mean?' he exclaimed.

'Talbot's the best-tempered fellow in the House.'

'Not at the moment!' grinned Cardew. 'Looks as if he's lost a fiver and found a farthing.'

'Rot!' growled Blake. And he went down the stairs to look for Talbot of the Shell in the junior day-room.

There was only one fellow in the day-room when Blake entered it. He was standing at the window, staring out into the misty winter gloom. He did not stir or turn his head as Blake came in.

'Talbot!' called out Blake, from the doorway.

Talbot did not seem to hear.

Blake crossed over to him.

'Talbot, old chap!' he exclaimed.

Then the Shell fellow looked round. The expression on his face startled the Fourth-former. His brows were darkly knitted, his lips set hard, and there was a restless glint in his eyes. He did not speak, but gave Blake a glance of impatient inquiry. Jack Blake eyed him, quite puzzled.

'Anything the matter, Talbot?' he asked.

'No — yes! What should be the matter?' muttered Talbot, and then turned back to the window and resumed his gloomy stare into the thickening gloom without.

'In a row with Railton for coming late?' asked Blake.

'No! No! Give a chap a rest.'

Blake frowned. He liked Talbot, as almost every fellow in the School House did: and almost every fellow in the New House, too. But he certainly did not like his manner at the moment.

'Well, you needn't bite a fellow's head off,' he said, tartly. 'I was looking for you. Didn't D'Arcy come in with you?'

'D'Arcy! No! I left him walking — the silly owl forgot to put a lamp on his bike,' said Talbot. 'D'Arcy all over. I expect he will wander in some time, if he doesn't take half a dozen wrong turnings one after another.'

Blake breathed rather hard.

'Did you lose anything while you were out on that spin with D'Arcy, Talbot?' he asked.

'Eh? No! Not that I know of.'

'I fancy you did,' said Blake.

Talbot stared round.

'What do you mean, Blake? What do you fancy I lost?'

'I fancied you might have lost your temper!' explained Blake, sarcastically. 'And you seem to have lost your civility along with it.'

'Oh, don't talk rot.'

Blake looked at him meditatively.

'We've been pretty good friends since you came

to St. Jim's, Talbot,' he said, 'so I won't punch your cheeky head. But you'll get it punched if you keep on asking for it like that.'

With that, Blake turned on his heel and walked out of the day-room. Talbot gave an impatient shrug of the shoulders and stared from the window again, the look on his handsome face growing darker and darker.

Blake tramped up the stairs again, back to Study No. 6. Herries and Dig, sitting down to prep, gave him inquiring looks as he came in.

'The ass hasn't a light on his bike, and he's walking it, Talbot says,' said Blake. 'Goodness knows when he will blow in.'

'Silly ass!' commented Herries.

'Gussy all over!' said Dig.

And the three started prep. It was considerably later that a footstep was heard outside Study No. 6 and the door opened. Arthur Augustus D'Arcy came wearily in.

'Oh! You've trickled in at last,' said Blake.

'Yaas, wathah.'

'Had a nice walk?' inquired Herries.

'Weally, Hewwies —'

'Railton rag you?' asked Blake.

'He did not exactly wag me, deah boy,' answered Arthur Augustus, 'but he has given me a hundwed lines. He seemed to think it was my fault somehow that I had to wheel my jiggah home.'

'And wasn't it?' asked Blake.

'Not at all, so fah as I can see,' said Arthur Augustus, warmly. 'We should have been back befoah dark, if I hadn't had that beastly puncture: and I should have wemembahed to stick the lamp on my jiggah, if I hadn't happened to forget it. I fail to see that I was to blame in any way. Howevah, it is no use twyin' to argue with a housebeak.'

'Have you been rowing with Talbot?' asked Dig.

'Certainly not.'

'Who's been tapping your boko, then?'

Arthur Augustus passed a hand over his noble nose. It was a good deal redder than usual, and seemed to have a pain in it.

'That was the wuffian,' he said.

'What ruffian?'

'I weally do not know, Blake, as I had nevah seen him befoah, and I twust I shall nevah see him again. He cut up wusty because I wan him down in Wayland Lane, and pitched into me in a perfectly fewocious mannah. It was not my fault weally, as I could not see him in the dark — and I suppose he could not see me, as I had no light on my jiggah —'

'You dangerous ass — riding without a light —!' exclaimed Blake.

'Weally, Blake —'

'Did he punch you hard?'

'Yaas, wathah, vewy hard indeed.'

'Good!' said Blake, heartily. 'You fathead, you might have been run in. Did you tell Railton you'd been riding without a light and knocking over people right and left?'

'I did not mention the mattah to Wailton, Blake. He would pwobably have thought that I was to blame.'

'Bank on that!' agreed Blake. 'You've got off cheap with a hundred lines. Now you'd better pile into prep, if you don't want Lathom to scalp you in the morning.'

'Bothah pwep!' sighed Arthur Augustus. 'I do not feel vewy much like pwep aftah pushin' that jiggah a mile and a half. As you fellows started first, you will be thwough befoah me: and pew-waps you would like to write my lines for me while I get thwough.'

'Perhaps!' grinned Blake.

'Lots of perhaps about that!' said Herries.

'As that Indian chap at Greyfriars would say, the perhapsfulness is terrific,' chuckled Dig.

'Oh, wats!' said Arthur Augustus.

He sat down to prep. Prep was an ordeal that had to be gone through: and Arthur Augustus went through it. He was still busy with it when Blake and Herries and Digby were through: and they left him to finish, with a hundred lines to follow.

CHAPTER V

A FRIEND IN NEED

'TALBOT!' exclaimed Tom Merry.

He stared into No. 9 in the Shell.

Prep was over. After prep, in No. 10, Monty Lowther had occupied some little time in telling his chums what he thought of a pair of wet blankets, who had no sense of humour, and who had spoiled what Monty persisted in regarding as a harmless and necessary jape on a house-beak. But for their fatheaded interference, Railton would have been hunting all over his study in search of bank-notes: only to find them parked under the cushion in his arm-chair: which, in Monty's opinion, would have been a real shriek! Tom Merry and Manners listened patiently: only occasionally interjecting 'Ass!' or 'Fathead!' However, Manners and Lowther had now gone down to the day-room: and Tom looked into No. 9 for Talbot. His few words with Talbot at the door of Mr. Railton's study had given him an uneasy impression that something was amiss with his friend: and now, as he looked into No. 9, he could have no doubt on that point. He was seated at the table, with his chin resting on his hand, his brows knitted, and an expression on his face of the deepest, darkest gloom.

He looked up quickly, as Tom uttered his name. The colour flushed into his face, and he rose abruptly to his feet.

'Oh! You!' he muttered.

'Talbot, old chap —'

'Leave me alone.'

'Wha-a-a-t?'

'I'd rather be left alone. I'm not coming down. You cut off.'

Tom Merry stared at him blankly. He set his lips a little.

'I'll cut off as soon as you like, Talbot,' he said. 'But —'

'Well, cut!'

Tom Merry paused in the doorway. Seldom, or never, did any fellow in the School House at St. Jim's get the 'rough edge' of Talbot's tongue. It had surprised Arthur Augustus D'Arcy in Wayland Lane: and it had surprised Jack Blake in the day-room. It more than surprised Tom Merry. Ever since the junior whose life had been so strangely chequered had come to St. Jim's, he had been

Talbot's best friend: and had stood by him in good times and bad — and there had been times when Talbot had sorely needed such a friend. Tom checked a momentary feeling of resentment.

He did not 'cut'. He came into the study, and closed the door after him. Talbot watched that action with unconcealed impatience.

'Look here, Talbot,' said Tom, quietly.

'I've said I want to be alone.'

'No other fellow would have to say it twice!' said Tom, in the same quiet tone. 'Look here, old man — what's wrong? I can see that there's something wrong — very wrong. What's the matter?'

Talbot made no reply to that.

'We're pals,' said Tom. 'You can trust me, I suppose? What on earth can have happened to put your back up like this?'

No answer.

'Surely you didn't lose your temper with Gussy, causing you to come in late? That wouldn't be like you.'

'Yes — no — oh, it's no use talking! You'd better leave me alone.'

'I'll do that fast enough if you really want it,' said Tom. 'But if there's some trouble — I might help —'

'You couldn't.'

'Then there is some trouble?

Talbot stood quite silent for a long minute, Tom's eyes on his dark, clouded face. The eyes of friendship were keen: and Tom could see that he was in the grip of a deep and black despondency: a depression deep and overwhelming. He could see, too, that Talbot was undergoing an inward struggle. It was a great relief to him to see the black look on the handsome face clear a little, at last.

'I'm sorry, Tom,' Talbot spoke quietly. 'I didn't mean to be surly — but — I've had a jolt — I don't know what to do.' He clenched his hands. 'I just don't know what to do — what I ought to do, or what I can do — I'm in a jam and I don't know the way out.'

'Can't you tell me?'

'If you like — but you can't help! Why should I land my wretched troubles on another fellow's shoulders?'

'Might help to get it off your chest. Brooding over troubles never does any good,' said Tom. 'But I'm dashed if I can guess what's up — any fellow would think you one of the lucky ones —'

'I!' exclaimed Talbot, staring.

'Yes, you,' said Tom. 'Good in form, good at games, popular in the House and the School — liked by everybody, trusted by everybody, with

more friends than you could count on your fingers
and toes —'

Talbot laughed harshly.

'Have you forgotten what I was, before I came
to St. Jim's?' he asked, bitterly. 'Have you forgotten that when I was a little kid, I fell among
thieves — that I was one of them, that I was
nicknamed the Toff, that I never had a chance of
going straight until I came to this school —'

'Don't speak of that!' said Tom, with a shiver.

'You're making me speak of it.'

'Oh!' A light broke on Tom. 'Is it something to
do with that — with the past that everyone here
has forgotten?'

'I haven't forgotten,' said Talbot. 'Sometimes
it seems like an unreal dream of long ago, and
I keep it out of my mind — but when I get a reminder —'

'You've had a reminder today?'

'Yes.'

Tom's face clouded.

'I understand, old chap,' he said softly, 'but —
what — ? What's happened?'

'I may as well tell you,' said Talbot, wearily.
'That ass D'Arcy — he forgot his lamp, and was
riding without a light, and he ran into a man —'
His brow darkened again. 'You see, he made me

ride on, and I left him walking — never thinking that he would be ass enough to ride without a lamp on his machine. But he did — and he crashed into a man and knocked him over —'

'The ass!' said Tom. 'But I don't see —'

'You will, when I tell you the rest,' muttered Talbot.

'Carry on, then,' said Tom.

'The man pitched into him and I was still near enough to hear the row, and I went back to help him. If only I hadn't —'

'Dash it all, you had to!' exclaimed Tom. 'Gussy was an ass, and he asked for a punch or two, but if he needed help —'

'The brute would have knocked him right out if I hadn't gone back. He was always an evil-tempered, malicious brute.'

Tom Merry started.

'You knew him?' he exclaimed.

'Not at first — but when the light fell on his face, I knew him! Smug Purkiss, the cracksman, one of the old gang in Angel Alley!' said Talbot, in a low voice.

'Oh!' said Tom.

'And he knew me — and called me by the name I'd half-forgotten and hoped never to hear again — the Toff!'

'Oh!' repeated Tom. 'Did D'Arcy hear —?'

'He must have — he may have told a dozen fellows by this time,' said Talbot, bitterly.

Tom Merry shook his head.

'Gussy's not the fellow to do that,' he said. 'He hasn't a lot of sense, but he has sense enough to know that you wouldn't want such things talked about. Bank on it that D'Arcy hasn't said a word on the subject.'

'It doesn't make much difference.'

'But what did you do?' asked Tom.

Talbot's eyes gleamed.

'Smug claimed me as an old acquaintance. He can't know anything about my being a schoolboy here now. I've no doubt that he fancies me still in the old line of business,' said Talbot. 'He's a little rat of a fellow — I could knock him side-ways — and I'd have done so if he hadn't cleared. He went at a run.'

'He's gone then?'

'Yes.'

'It's rotten, old chap, to have the past dragged up by a chance meeting like that,' said Tom, 'but you're hardly likely to see him again.'

'No!'

'He doesn't know you're here?'

'He cannot.'

'Even if he knew, he has no hold on you?'

'None.'

'If that's all, then —'

Talbot breathed very hard.

'If that were all, Tom, I could throw it out of my mind, and have done with it. But that's not all.'

'What else?' asked Tom.

'Even D'Arcy isn't idiot enough to run a man down on the road, light or no light. He ran into the man, because he dropped suddenly from the park wall of Wayland Grange. What was Smug Purkiss doing inside the walls of Wayland Grange after dark, Tom?'

'Oh!' said Tom.

'And he's a cracksman — one of the cunningest cracksmen in the old gang,' said Talbot. 'And Wayland Grange the home of Sir Josiah Billing, the richest man in this part of Sussex.'

Tom's face became very grave.

'You think he was there for a robbery?' he asked.

'Not so early — Smug's is a midnight game,' answered Talbot. 'But I know the routine. He was there to mug up the lie of the lane, so that he would have his bearings when he came later for the safe. Nothing could have happened yet — but something's scheduled to happen — perhaps tonight —

perhaps some other night — Smug was not there
for nothing, Tom.'

'I understand,' said Tom, slowly.

'Now you see how I'm fixed!' muttered Talbot.
'It's as good as certain that old Billing's place has
been marked down for Smug's next job. What can
I do? I can't let it go on —'

'You can't!' said Tom, decidedly.

'But what can I do?' muttered Talbot. 'If I do
nothing there'll be a burglary at Wayland Grange
— but if I do anything, it means the old wretched
story dragged up again — the Toff, the Angel Alley
gang — and the rest of it — the old story I've
tried to forget and almost everyone else has forgotten. Talbot of the Shell with such acquaintances
as Smug Purkiss, gangster and cracksman —' He
shuddered.

Tom Merry stood silent.

'You see, you can't help, old fellow,' said Talbot. 'You'd much better have left me alone — I've
got to wrestle this out somehow on my own. I —
I almost wish I'd never come to St. Jim's at all —'

'That's rot,' said Tom.

'A fellow can't shake off the past,' said Talbot,
moodily. 'It clings like a shadow.' He set his lips.
'If that ass D'Arcy hadn't run into the man —
I should have known nothing — never dreamed

that Smug was in Sussex at all — I'd forgotten his existence. Now I know —'

'Do you want me to tell you what I think?' asked Tom.

Talbot shrugged his shoulders.

'Go ahead — if you're not sick of me and my rotten associations,' he said.

'Don't be an ass, old chap,' said Tom. 'I'm glad you've told me, because I think I can help. It was a spot of luck D'Arcy running into the man, if you look at it the right way.'

'What?'

'It's put you wise,' said Tom. 'You know now that that rascal is around and you know what his game is. You can give warning —'

'I can walk into Wayland Grange and tell them that an old acquaintance of mine is planning to crack the safe?' said Talbot, with bitter sarcasm. 'Is that the idea? Thanks!'

'That isn't the idea,' said Tom. 'You're upset now, old chap, and looking at the worst side of things. You've got a plain duty to do: and no harm ever came to a fellow for doing his duty. Inspector Skeat at Wayland knows your story, knows it from beginning to end. Police officers are mum as oysters — whatever you may tell him will go no further. There will be no need to mention your

name and he will not mention it. The police act on
what they call "information received" without giving away the source.'

'But —!' muttered Talbot.

'You can get him on the phone,' said Tom. 'Tell
him, plainly, that a man you know to be a cracksman is hanging about Wayland Grange. That will
be enough for Mr. Skeat. The rest is up to him.'

Talbot stood looking at him in silence.

'Skeat will be jolly glad to get the tip, and he
will take whatever measures seem to him proper,
as a police-inspector,' said Tom. 'You won't come
into the picture at all, old chap.'

Talbot drew a deep breath.

'As simple as that!' he muttered.

'Just as simple as that,' said Tom. 'You've had
a jolt, old fellow, and you've let it get you down —
but it's as simple as that. Mr. Skeat will take jolly
good care to put paid to Smug Purkiss, if he shows
up at the Grange, and you can chuck the whole
thing out of your mind.'

Talbot's face broke into a smile.

'I'm glad you came in, Tom,' he said. 'There's
an old proverb that a friend in need is a friend
indeed. I could never have pulled through at St.
Jim's at all, Tom, without you — and now —'

'Now you've got to scout round and bag a

telephone!' said Tom, smiling too. 'And then forget it all, old fellow: and next time a pal drops into your study, you won't bite his head off.'

'Oh! Tom! I'm sorry —'

'Speech taken as read,' said Tom, laughing. 'Come on, old boy — the beaks will be in Common-Room now, and I'll keep cave while you bag a phone —'

They left No. 9 study together. On the landing they passed Cardew of the Fourth, who glanced at Talbot with a grin. But Talbot of the Shell was no longer looking like a bear with a sore head! His face was bright as he went down the stairs with Tom Merry.

CHAPTER VI

HARD LINES!

'WOTTEN!' sighed Arthur Augustus D'Arcy.

He was beginning on his hundred lines.

His Virgil was propped open on the table before him. His pen was in his hand. A sheet of impot paper was ready. But the verse of Publius Virgilius Maro seemed to have no attraction for him.

He had to write out from 'Defessi Aeneadae' to 'dehinc talia fatur': and he had to hand the lines in before dorm. A long bike spin, a walk of a mile and a half, and an interview with his house-master, and prep, had somewhat tired the swell of St. Jim's: and he was quite disinclined to cover the impot paper with transcribed Latin.

However, there was no help for it: and he dipped his pen in the ink and started. It was not unknown for fellows to help one another with lines: and Arthur Augustus would have been glad of contributions from Blake and Herries and Dig. But Blake, Herries and Dig had a boxing match on after prep with Levison, Clive and Cardew of the Fourth: and that was that. Alone in his study, Arthur Augustus sadly wrote 'defessi Aeneadae, quae proxima litora, cursu' and then paused for a rest.

'Busy?'

It was a cheerful voice in the study doorway.

Arthur Augustus looked round. But he did not bestow a welcoming look on the handsome Shell fellow standing in the doorway. His glance at Talbot of the Shell was icy.

'Yaas!' he said, briefly. And he dropped his eyes to his imposition, and dipped his pen in the ink again.

'Sorry to interrupt —!' said Talbot.

'There is no occasion for you to intewwupt, Talbot!' answered Arthur Augustus, over his shoulder. 'Pway, wun along.'

'Lines?' asked Talbot.

'Yaas.'

Talbot came into the study. Arthur Augustus did not look up, but a slight frown corrugated his aristocratic brow.

'I wanted to speak to you, D'Arcy,' said Talbot, amicably.

'The want is entiahly on your side, Talbot,' answered Arthur Augustus, stiffly. 'I pwefer to say nothin' to you.' Arthur Augustus lifted his

noble head, and fixed a severe look on his visitor.
'You have pewwaps forgotten, Talbot, that you
addwessed me in a vewy wude mannah in Wayland Lane! I wegwet to say that I have no use for
wudeness, Talbot. I pwefer to dwop your acquaintance.'

'But I came in to say —'

'Nevah mind what you came in to say. Pway
wun along and leave me to do my lines.'

'To say that I'm sorry I cut up rusty, D'Arcy—'

'Oh!' Arthur Augustus's frowning brow relaxed.

'I was a bit upset, old fellow. I-I-I suppose you
heard what that man said to me.' Talbot's look was
a little anxious.

'I could scarcely help hearin' what you heard,
Talbot, as I was just as neah the bwute as you were.'

'Oh! Quite! And you heard me call him by
name.'

'Natuwally.'

'If you've not mentioned it to anyone so far, I'd
rather you didn't,' said Talbot.

'Weally, Talbot —' Arthur Augustus laid down
his pen. 'I have told Blake and Hewwies and Dig
about what happened in Wayland Lane, but I have
certainly not mentioned that the person — that
vewy unpleasant person — appeahed to be an old
acquaintance of yours.'

'You see —!' muttered Talbot. 'I wouldn't like a thing like that to become the talk of the day-room.'

'I twust, Talbot, that you can wely on my tact and judgement in such a mattah,' said Arthur Augustus, with dignity. 'I am vewy well awah that you would not like that old stowy waked up: and I nevah even dweamed of mentionin' to my fwiends that you appeahed to know the man and called him by the vewy wemarkable name of Pug —'

'Not Pug!' said Talbot.

'Or Slug, or whatevah it was,' said Arthur Augustus. 'I weally quite forget what it was exactly — Pug or Slug or Chug or somethin'. Neithah have I wefened to the circumstance that he addwessed you by a nickname. It is not my business, Talbot, and I have dismissed the whole mattah fwom my mind. And if you are satisfied upon that point, Talbot, pewwaps you will wun along and let me finish these wotten lines for Wailton.'

'I've something else to say —'

'Weally, Talbot —'

'I've said I'm sorry, old fellow. I was a bit knocked over, and upset, and — and — and I apologise.'

Arthur Augustus's noble brow cleared completely.

'Bai Jove! If you put it like that, Talbot —'

'I do put it exactly like that!' said Talbot, solemnly.

'Then it is all wight!' said Arthur Augustus, reassuringly. 'Fwom one gentleman to anothah, an apology sets evewythin' wight. Pway forget all about it, deah boy. Wash it wight out.'

'Good!' said Talbot.

'But you must wun along all the same,' added Arthur Augustus. 'I have to hand in a hundwed lines before the bell goes for dorm.'

'Hard luck,' said Talbot. 'But —'

'Did Wailton give you lines?' asked Arthur Augustus.

Talbot shook his head.

'No. He made allowance for that puncture,' Talbot smiled. 'Of course, I could have pushed on and left you to handle the puncture on your own: but Railton wouldn't expect a fellow to do that. He's a good sort.'

'Yaas, wathah, but I weally wish he had been a little more weasonable with me, too,' said Arthur Augustus. 'He seemed to think that I was to blame somehow for not havin' a light on my jiggah. He couldn't weally think that I forgot to stick a lamp on intentionally: but he gave me a hundwed lines all the same. And I've got to gwind them out be-

foah dorm,' added Arthur Augustus, and he dipped
his pen in the ink again.

'Let me help,' suggested Talbot.

Arthur Augustus brightened.

'Bai Jove! If you'd like to do a few, Talbot —'

'More than a few.'

'Pewwaps you might do twenty!'

'Fifty-fifty,' said Talbot. 'You begin, and I'll
carry on from the middle. Where are you starting?'

'Defessi Aeneadae —'

Talbot picked up Virgil and turned the pages.

'Then I'll begin at "durate et vosmet" — just in
the middle of the hundred,' said Talbot. 'Race you
to the finish, old man.'

Arthur Augustus laughed.

'Wight-ho!' he said.

Talbot sat down at the table, picked up Blake's
pen, and started. Arthur Augustus re-started in
a much more cheerful mood. Fifty lines was quite
as much as he wanted: his task was halved.

They sat and wrote Latin lines. Talbot was
a quick worker and he had arrived at 'dehinc talia
fatur' by the time Arthur Augustus was half-way
through fifty. He sat, pen in hand.

Arthur Augustus looked up.

'Bai Jove! Thwough alweady, old chap?' he
asked.

'I'd bettah do a few more,' said Talbot.

'That would be wathah wisky,' said Arthur Augustus, with a shake of the head. 'Wailton hardly looks at a fellow's lines: but we won't ovahdo it, old boy. I wouldn't like to get you into a wow for helpin' me out. Beaks,' added Arthur Augustus, with another shake of the head, 'beaks don't look at these mattahs as we do, Talbot. Wailton would be watty if he knew that a fellow did anothah fellow's lines.'

'Oh! Yes! But —'

'And I am bound to say,' continued Arthur Augustus, 'that fwom their point of view, they are quite wight. It weally isn't much use givin' a fellow lines if anothah fellow does them for him. Of course, between ourselves, it is as wight as wain. But you have to be wary with beaks.'

'Oh! quite!' said Talbot, smiling. 'I'll leave you to finish them, then.'

'Yaas, wathah! Thank you vewy much for doin' half my lines, Talbot — it was weally fwightfully decent of you, deah boy. And — Oh, cwikey!'

Arthur Augustus broke off, quite suddenly, as the study door, which Talbot had left ajar, was pushed open, and a figure in cap and gown appeared there. His noble jaw dropped as he stared at his house-master — too startled even to rise to his feet.

Talbot caught his breath.

'I heard what you said, D'Arcy, as I was passing your door!' said Mr. Railton, very quietly.

'Oh, cwumbs!'

'Talbot!'

'Yes sir!' said Talbot, in a low voice.

'I cannot,' said Mr. Railton, in the same quiet tone, 'take official note of words heard by chance, spoken inadvertently in my hearing, otherwise I should deal with you severely, Talbot. You are not a foolish, thoughtless boy like D'Arcy —'

'Weally, Mr. Wailton —'

'Silence! You are well aware, Talbot, that you have broken a strict rule of the House and the School.'

Talbot was silent. He was well enough aware of it. He was aware, too, that as Arthur Augustus had said, 'beaks' did not look at such matters as school-boys did.

'I shall say nothing more, Talbot, except that I am extremely displeased with you!' said Mr. Railton.

With that, the house-master walked on.

'Bai Jove!' said Arthur Augustus, faintly. 'I am aw'fly sowwy, Talbot, deah boy — I seem to have landed you in a wow.'

'Okay,' said Talbot, as lightly as he could. 'Push on with your lines, old boy. Cheerio.'

Talbot left the study with a cheery smile and nod. But his face clouded when the door of Study No. 6 had closed on him.

CHAPTER VII

A TALK ON THE TELEPHONE

'MERRY!'

Tom Merry glanced round.

'Yes, sir!'

It was the following day. The 'Terrible Three' were sauntering in the quad after dinner, chatting — on rather varied topics. Tom's remarks chiefly concerned the Soccer match shortly due with the New House. Manners was thinking more of his camera, and whether the wintry sunlight was quite suitable for taking a few snaps with the same. Monty Lowther interjected remarks on the subject of wet blankets who spoiled a jolly good jape on a beak! This triangular conversation was interrupted by the voice of Mr. Linton, the master of the Shell, calling to Tom from his study window, which the three Shell fellows were passing at the moment.

Tom turned towards the window as he answered the call.

'Merry, please find Talbot and tell him to come to my study,' said Mr. Linton.

'Yes, sir!'

'You may tell him that someone desires to speak to him on the telephone, and is holding the line.'

'Very well, sir.'

Leaving Manners and Lowther to continue their discussion of cameras and wet blankets, Tom hurried away in search of Talbot. He found him strolling under the old elms, with a thoughtful and somewhat clouded brow.

'Anything up, old chap?' asked Tom. He could see that something was troubling Talbot's mind.

'Oh! Not exactly,' answered Talbot, with a faint smile. 'Nothing much —'

'Not still worrying about that affair yesterday?'

'Oh! No! That's over and done with,' said Talbot. 'You gave me good advice, Tom, and I did exactly as you said. I wasn't thinking of that. But —'

'But what, then?'

'Nothing much — only Railton caught me helping D'Arcy with his lines last evening and he was shirty.' Talbot coloured, 'It's nothing really — but — but — Railton has always been so jolly kind to me, and he's such a good sort — I hate to displease him even in the slightest way. Of course, fellows shouldn't do as I was doing —'

'Fellows often do,' said Tom.

'Yes, but — but it's strictly against the rules, as Railton said.'

Tom Merry smiled.

'Beaks often forget that they were once school-boys themselves,' he said. 'But I was looking for you to tell you that you're wanted, Talbot. Linton's study. You're wanted on the phone.'

Talbot started.

'On the phone! Surely Skeat wouldn't ring me up about what I told him yesterday — he knows I wouldn't want any talk here —'

'Not likely,' answered Tom. 'Might be a call from your uncle, Colonel Lyndon. Anyhow you'd better cut off and take it — Linton said that who-ever it was, was holding the line.'

Talbot nodded, and walked away quickly to the School House. Mr. Linton's door was open when he arrived: the master of the Shell had left his study. The telephone receiver was off the hooks, and Talbot crossed over quickly to the instrument and picked it up.

'Hallo! Talbot speaking!' he said into the trans-mitter.

'You, Toff?' came a chuckling voice.

Talbot almost dropped the receiver in his sur-prise. It was the voice of Smug Purkiss that came through.

'You!' he breathed.

'Jest me, Toff, rung you up for a little chat.'

Talbot set his lips. His brow was black as he answered:

'You rascal! You skulking rascal! How dare you ring me up here, at my school?'

'Can't a covey ring up an old friend?' came a chuckle.

'You never were a friend of mine, you rat! Even in those days, when I was no better than you perhaps, I drew a line at a skulking rogue like you,' said Talbot in a low voice of concentrated scorn.

'You was always 'igh and mighty, even when you was known to the police as the cutest cracksman going, boy as you was!' chuckled Smug. 'But come off it, Toff — I got to talk to you. If you'd rather I walked into your school to see you, jest say so, and I'll come.'

Talbot shivered.

'How did you know I was here?' he asked, controlling his anger and indignation. 'How could you know even my name?'

'I got my wits about me, Toff. Didn't I 'ear that young cove who ran me down on his bike, call you Talbot? A noo name for you, Toff — quite a nice one you've picked out!' Smug chuckled again. 'And you was wearing a St. Jim's cap and so was

he — and I been long enough around these parts
to know one when I see one! I'm telling you, Toff,
that you could have knocked me over with a feather
when I got it that you was playing schoolboy at
a big public school under a noo name! Strike me
pink! What's your game at St. Jim's, Toff?'

Talbot breathed hard.

'That's why you cut up so rusty, what?' went
on the mocking voice. 'You didn't want that young
covey to know anything about your old acquaintances! You're on a new lay, Toff, and you got to
go wary, what?'

Talbot did not reply. He stood with the receiver
in his hand, his brow black, his eyes glinting.

His right hand clenched almost convulsively.
Had the mocking rascal at the other end been
within reach, it would have gone hard with him. It
was fortunate for Mr. Purkiss that there was a
telephone-line between.

'Don't you panic, Toff!' went on the chuckling
voice. 'I ain't giving an old pal away. I ain't butting
into your game at the school, whatever it is. The
head-master's safe, what?'

'You villain!' breathed Talbot.

'Go easy, old covey!' chuckled Smug. 'I s'pose
you ain't at school to learn Latin and geography,
what? You're on a lay.'

Talbot panted. That, the realised, was the view a rogue like Purkiss would take: he could only suppose that the one-time Toff, the one-time boy-cracksman who had a magic hand with a safe, was on a 'lay', as he called it.

'I tell you, it beat me, when I worked it out where you was, and what you was up to,' went on Smug, as Talbot did not speak. 'I'd 'ardly believed it, and I put through this call to make sure. I rings up the school and asks to be put through to Master Talbot, jest to try it on. See? I wasn't sure till I 'eard your voice come through.' Smug chuckled again.

'You were put through to my form-master who allowed me to take the call,' said Talbot, speaking at last. 'Perhaps it's just as well — we can get it clear! I am not here on a lay, Smug.'

'Sez you!'

'I am here as a schoolboy, like the rest. I threw over the old life at the first chance and since then I've never looked back. Can you understand that? The Toff is dead and done with: I am Talbot of the Shell, and nothing else.'

'And they knows all about you?' came a derisive chuckle.

'Everything is known and forgiven,' said Talbot, quietly. 'I was given a chance here: and I made

the most of it: I am trusted by my head-master
and house-master, and by everyone who has heard
my story. You cannot do me any harm here, Smug!
If you came here and shouted out my whole history
at the top of your voice it would make no difference.'

'Strike me pink!'

'Now you know how the matter stands,' said
Talbot, 'and now I have had a word with you,
I will tell you one thing more. Your best guess is
to get out of this neighbourhood at once.'

'You'd like to see the last of an old pal!' chuckled
Smug.

'That is true! But that is not all! Do you think
I do not know why you were lurking at Wayland
Grange yesterday after dark?'

'I reckoned you'd guess.'

'I did guess! And I have tipped the local police.

'Wha-a-at?'

'Inspector Skeat of Wayland Police Station
knows now that Smug Purkiss, convict and cracksman, is hanging about, with an eye on Wayland
Grange!' said Talbot, quietly. 'It won't be healthy
for you to crack that crib, Smug.'

'You — a copper's nark!' came a hiss of fury
over the wires. 'You give me away to the cops —'

'I've put paid to your rascality!' said Talbot.

'Get out while the going's good — that's your best guess.'

'You want me to believe that you're going straight — that you, a magician at cracking a safe, have chucked it over — and become a schoolboy — you want me to believe that?'

'You can believe what you like,' said Talbot contemptuously. 'But that is exactly how the matter stands. Any more before I cut off?'

He heard the man panting at the other end

'Look 'ere Toff —'

'That will do!'

'You got to 'ear me! I got to talk to you, Toff. We got to settle things. You come out of your school and see me —'

'I will do nothing of the kind.'

'I'll wait for you — you know the old hut in the wood, near the Wayland footpath — I'll wait there —'

'You'll wait for nothing.'

'You won't come?'

'No!'

'Then you'll see me at your school! I'll come to the school and talk to you! You'd like that better?'

Talbot set his teeth.

'Do you mean that, Smug?'

'Every word.'

'Very well,' said Talbot, between his teeth. 'If I've got to see you, Smug, I'd rather see you out of gates. I'll come along to the old hut this afternoon. I can get out after class. Wait for me at four.'

'That's a go, Toff.'

'I'd rather not come! I'd rather you went quietly, and left me in peace. Will you do that, Purkiss?'

'Can it!' came the jeering reply. 'You turn up, like you've said, if you don't want to see me walking into your school.'

'Very well!' said Talbot. 'I shall be there! That's all!' He hung up the receiver, and if Smug answered he did not hear him.

He hurried out of the study, glad to go before Mr. Linton returned. His face was set, his eyes glinting: and if Smug Purkiss had seen that look on his face, he might have regretted that the appointment had been made at the old hut in Wayland Wood. For whatever Smug Purkiss expected from that meeting, it was what he did not expect that was going to happen — he had forced Talbot to consent to see him, and the outcome was going to be the soundest thrashing that Mr. Purkiss had ever received in the whole course of his rascally life!

CHAPTER VIII

WARNED OFF

"'ERE you are, Toff!"

Smug Purkiss grinned as he spoke.

He was lounging in the old hut in the wood, smoking one cigarette after another, while he waited for the Shell fellow of St. Jim's. The hut, once used by woodmen, was old and falling into ruins. It was not far from the footpath that ran from the Wayland road to Rylcombe Lane: but it was solitary, hidden by trees and thickets, and quite a safe place for a secret meeting, for it was seldom or never visited. It suited Mr. Purkiss whose ways were stealthy, and who preferred to keep out of the general view when he was on a 'lay'. He smoked and waited, and at length he heard a rustle in the underwoods, and a St. Jim's cap appeared in view. The set expression on Talbot's face, as he came towards the open doorway of the hut, rather amused Mr. Purkiss. He had, or fancied he had, the upper hand and he liked to use it. The more the 'Toff' resented it, the more

Smug liked making the boy, whom he had always disliked, dance to his tune. Talbot did not want to see him: but he had no doubt that the Toff would come: and now he was coming.

Talbot stepped into the hut.

'Here I am!' he assented quietly.

'We got to talk,' said Smug. 'Look 'ere, Toff —' he grinned as he repeated that name, and saw Talbot wince. 'Look 'ere, we was never friends, like you said, in the old days when you was in Captain Crow's gang with Hookey Walker and the Professor and the rest — but we worked together once or twice all the same, and we can do the same agin.'

Talbot looked at him in silence.

It was like an evil dream to him, to remember that once it had been as the gangster said. Looking back, he could hardly believe that it had been real. The gang had used him — his strange, almost uncanny skill with locks, had made him useful to them: from childhood he had been hopelessly entangled in evil associations. But escape had come — escape and a new life. All he wanted now was to forget what had been: and the mere sight of a face from the past was like a blow to him. His loathing for the grinning rascal before him was almost too deep for words.

'Cards on the table, Toff,' went on Smug. 'With your 'and with a safe, you got a fortune if you choose to pick it up: you ain't asking me to believe that you've throwed it all away to play at being a schoolboy.'

'You wouldn't understand,' said Talbot, wearily. 'I am a schoolboy now and nothing else, whatewer I once was. Since my uncle found me, he has paid my fees at school: and I am a schoolboy at St. Jim's like any other. I have nothing to do with you, and you have nothing to do with me.'

'Sez you!' sneered Smug. 'Look 'ere, Toff, let's talk sense. You know I'm on a lay 'ere — Wayland Grange —'

'I know! So does Inspector Skeat at Wayland.'

Smug's eyes glittered like a rat's.

'You give the game away to the cops, because you don't want an old acquaintance around while you play your own game at the school!' he muttered.

Talbot shrugged his shoulders contemptuously.

'Cannot you understand that I have no game at the school — excepting football,' he added.

'Talk sense!' snarled Smug. 'We ain't been friends, but we've worked together afore, and can agin. Look 'ere. Look 'ere, Toff. There's big money at Wayland Grange. I've had a look at the office.

There's a safe to be cracked there, with thousands.'

'I've no doubt of it.'

'Ours for the picking up!' said Smug.

'Ours!' repeated Talbot.

'We go in together,' said Smug eagerly. 'I ain't bearing malice for that jolt last night, Toff, so long as we work together. I'm telling you there's thousands — more'n enough for a divvy between pals. I ain't got your hand with a safe, and never had. What'd take me a couple of hours to work through, you'd open like it was a can with a can-opener. You ain't forgotten your skill, Toff, since you been a schoolboy. You was a prize-packet when you was in the gang.'

Talbot shuddered. He did not speak. The man went on eagerly.

'If I'd known you was around, I'd have got you to go in with me from the start, Toff! Now we've met, let's fix it up. Easy enough for you to get out of your school at night, with everybody asleep. The Toff always moved like he was a ghost.' Smug chuckled. 'I got that safe at the Grange marked down, Toff — but — it's risky — more risky now if you've given the cops the office. But with you along, it would be a matter of minutes. You know that, Toff.'

'I know it!' muttered Talbot.

'Is it a go, then?' breathed Smug.

Talbot looked at him. The man did not believe in his reform; such a belief could not lodge in his evil mind. To him the boy was still the 'Toff' of old: the young cracksman with a magic hand with a safe.

'It's thousands!' breathed Smug.

'Listen to me,' Talbot spoke very quietly. 'All that is dead and gone, Purkiss. I know without your telling me that I could crack the safe at Wayland Grange and handle thousands of pounds in a matter of minutes: leaving no clue. At my school I have the same amount of pocket money as the other fellows in my form: and I count it in shillings, not in pounds. And I prefer it that way, and it will stay that way. Not to handle thousands, not to save my life, would I touch a sixpence not my own. Try to get that into your head, Smug.'

Smug Purkiss stood watching his face as he spoke. His own face darkened with vindictive rage. It was borne in upon his mind, at last, that the boy was telling him the simple truth.

He spat out an oath.

'So the Toff's gone soft!' he sneered.

'Call it that if you like!' said Talbot. 'But that's how it is, Smug, and that's how it will stay. I've nothing to do with you and your ways — and all

I want from you is that you leave me alone, go
your way, and forget that you have seen me.'

Smug gritted his teeth.

'Likely!' he sneered. 'From what you've told me,
you've queered my pitch at the Grange. Mebbe
I could queer yours at the school.'

'You can do me no harm,' said Talbot, 'but I do
not choose to have you come to St. Jim's, Smug, and
remind them of what I want to be forgotten. I'm
asking you to go away and forget me.'

'Ask all you want!' jeered Smug. 'But look out
for me walking into your school tomorrow, and
giving you away to the whole crowd, Toff.'

Talbot drew a deep breath.

'You mean that?' he asked.

'You'll see, Toff.'

'You would be thrown out if you came.'

'I'll chance that!' jeered Smug.

'Very well,' said Talbot. 'I came here, Smug,
to make it clear to you that your best guess is to
go. You won't go — and you plan to make a scene
at my school, and make things unpleasant for me.
I'm going to thrash you, Smug — thrash you so
hard that you'll be glad to crawl away and keep
away. I'd rather you went in peace: but you're
going anyway — I'm going to give you the thrashing of your life, Smung — and the same again if

ever I set eyes on you anywhere near my school.'

Talbot spoke very quietly, but grimly. He pushed back his cuffs as he was speaking. There was no doubt that he meant to be as good as his word.

Smug backed way.

'Hands off!' he muttered. 'Look 'ere, Toff —'

'You've asked for it,' said Talbot. 'You won't take no for an answer. Now stand up to it! You're a man, and I'm a boy — pluck up your courage, you rat, and stand up to it.'

He came at the gangster as he spoke, his fists up, his eyes gleaming like steel over them. Smug Purkiss spat like a cat with rage: but there was no help for it: and his hands flew up in defence. The next moment they were fighting fiercely, furiously.

Smug Purkiss was a little man: but he was, after all, as Talbot had said, a man; and Talbot, strong and sturdy as he was, was only a schoolboy. And Smug was wiry and muscular. The advantage should have been on his side. But there was a yellow streak in Smug: and vindictive rage could not supply the place of courage. For several long minutes, Smug stood up to it, and his savage blows came home on Talbot's handsome face: but all the while the Shell fellow of St. Jim's was hitting, and hitting hard, putting all his force into every jolt that landed on the gangster. He had to take punishment: but he hardly heeded it: with set face and glinting eyes he attacked all the time, and Smug Purkiss was knocked right and left. Again and again he came at Talbot like a cat, only to reel under the lashing fists: and at length Smug could stand no more, and he went down under a terrific drive — and stayed down.

Talbot, panting, looked down at him.

Smug lay on his elbow, his eyes glittering up at Talbot like a rat's. The crimson was streaming from his nose: both his eyes were darkening — his breath came in gasps. He could have gone on: but all the 'thousands' in the safe at Wayland Grange would not have tempted him to rise and face those lashing fists again. He mumbled and groaned as he lay.

'Is that enough?' said Talbot, quietly. 'Enough to warn you, off, Smug?'

A panting oath was the answer.

'Keep clear of me,' said Talbot. 'That's all I want — keep clear! You've got what you asked for: and if ever I see you again, you'll get the same — and harder, Smug. Don't let me see you.'

'I'll remember this, Toff!' breathed Smug, thickly.

'Do!' said Talbot, contemptuously.

With that, he turned and walked out of the hut.

Smug Purkiss did not 'walk into' St. Jim's the following day, as he had threatened. And in the days that followed, Talbot of the Shell saw nothing and heard nothing of him. That drastic warning at the old hut in Wayland Wood seemed to have been enough for Smug: and he did not want another of the same. Perhaps, for a few days, Talbot felt a lingering uneasiness that the gangster might still be hanging about the vicinity: and he was prepared to deal with him even more drastically if it proved to be so. But the days passed: and he was satisfied at last that Smug was gone. His 'lay' at Wayland Grange was too risky, since Inspector Skeat had been put on the alert: there had been no news of any attempt on Sir Josiah's safe at that mansion. No doubt the gangster had gone seething with rage and resentment: but for that Talbot cared nothing. He was gone: and the Shell fellow of St. Jim's was able, at last, to dismiss him from mind.

CHAPTER IX

A MYSTERY OF THE NIGHT

ARTHUR AUGUSTUS D'ARCY stirred uneasily in his sleep.

His eyes opened in the dimness of the Fourth-form dormitory in the School House.

The hour was late. Midnight had boomed dully through the wintry night. It was very unusual for Arthur Augustus's eyes to open at such an hour. Generally the swell of St. Jim's slept like a top. But Arthur Augustus was not in his usual serene state that night. The House-match had been played that afternoon, and Arthur Augustus, in the front line for his House, had captured a goal, which was satisfactory, and a hack on his noble knee, which was extremely unsatisfactory. Not that Gussy was the man to make a fuss about an accidental hard knock in a Soccer game. He bore it with cheerful equanimity. But it was painful, and it made his slumber uneasy. Several times that night, while every other fellow in the dormitory was fast asleep, Arthur Augustus had awakened: and now he had

awakened again, with a throbbing twinge in that
painful knee.

He sat up in bed and gave that knee a rub.

Then he gave a little jump.

The dormitory was dark: there was scarcely a
glimmer at the high windows. The darkness should
naturally have been unbroken. But, to D'Arcy's
startled surprise, a glimmer of light broke it.

He stared blankly at that glimmer.

He knew what it was: the gleam of a small
electric torch. And as he stared at it in wonder, it
moved and moved again. Whoever was carrying
it was moving about the dormitory.

'Bai Jove!' breathed Arthur Augustus, inaudibly.

Silent, staring, he watched the moving light.

He saw it stop beside Blake's bed, but only for
a moment. Then it moved on again, and stopped
at Digby's. Then it moved on to Herries' bed, and
then to Levison's, then to Clive's, then to Cardew's,
then to Trimble's.

In utter amazement, D'Arcy watched it.

He could see nothing of the person who held the
light, hidden in darkness behind it. Whoever it
was, was stepping silently to bed after bed, apparently to direct the light for a second on the
sleepers in turn, as if in search of one particular
individual.

Unless it was some fellow from another dormitory, bent on a 'lark' in the middle of the night, Arthur Augustus could not begin to guess what it meant. Such 'larks' sometimes occurred. There were fellows like Monty Lowther, of the Shell, who were too funny to live: and there had been an occasion when Arthur Augustus had found his trousers sewn up in the morning, and had had no doubt that he owed that kindly attention to the funny man of the Shell. If this was that funny ass japing again —

The glimmer of light approached D'Arcy's own bed.

Japer or not, Monty Lowther or not, the unknown holder of the light was coming with noiseless tread, to give him the once-over in his turn.

Arthur Augustus's brow knitted grimly.

It was a painful throb in his bruised knee that had awakened him: but he was glad now that he had awakened. He groped for his pillow, and took a firm grip on it.

Whiz!

The pillow flew through the air. Arthur Augustus aimed at the light: all that he could see of the mysterious midnight visitor. His aim was good. There was a crash, as the whizzing missile struck, taking the intruder utterly by surprise. The light

went out: and all was dark, but Arthur Augustus
knew that the intruder had been knocked over, and
was sprawling on his back on the floor.

He heard a gasping breath from the darkness.

'Got you, you japin' wottah!' chuckled Arthur
Augustus. 'Blake — Hewwies — Dig — wake up,
you fellows! Collah him!'

He bounded out of bed.

There were voices from the other beds at once.
The crash of the intruder's fall, followed by Arthur
Augustus's excited shout, was more than enough
to rouse the whole dormitory.

'Hallo, what's up?' came Blake's voice.

'What's the row —'

'Is that D'Arcy — ?'

'You silly ass, what are you up to?'

'Turn out, you fellows!' yelled Arthur Augustus.
'Don't let the wottah get away without a waggin!'

He plunged, in the darkness, in the direction of
the fallen intruder, groping for him in the gloom.
But his groping hands met only empty space.
Whoever it was that had intruded into the Fourth-
form dormitory, had moved quickly. He was gone
before Arthur Augustus reached the spot.

'You burbling ass!' came Cardew's voice. 'What
are you waking us all up for at this time of night?'

'Weally, Cardew —'

'Can't you go to sleep, and let other fellows go to sleep, image?' howled Jack Blake.

'I wefuse to be called an image, Blake! There is somebody in the dorm —'

'There's all of us in the dorm, fathead!'

'I mean there is somebody else, Blake — some japin' ass fwom anothah dormitory. I have no doubt that it is that funny ass Lowthah. You wemembah that he sewed up my twousahs one night —'

'Ha, ha, ha!'

'It is not a laughin' mattah to sew up a fellow's twousahs! Turn out and collah him and wag him!' shouted Arthur Augustus.

'Oh, all right — if there's anybody!' grunted Blake. Evidently Blake had doubts whether there was anybody!

A light gleamed out, as Levison lighted a candle-end. He held it up, and it cast a glimmer through the long dark dormitory. Arthur Augustus found his pillow and picked it up, prepared to handle it as a weapon for offence as soon as he spotted the intruder.

But he stared in all directions, without picking up a sign of that intruder. Blake and Herries and Digby, Levison and Clive and Cardew, Dick Julian and Harry Hammond, and several other fellows, turned out of bed. If some japer from another

dormitory was there, bent on larking in the middle
of the night, they were ready to make him properly
sorry for himself.

But they failed to find any sign of him. Blake
switched on the light and the dormitory was illu-
minated from end to end. But the light did not
reveal any intruder from without.

'You silly ass!' said Blake, in measured tones.
'You burbling bandersnatch, if there's somebody
here, where is he?'

'Weally, Blake —'

'Where is he, fathead?' hooted Herries.

'Weally, Hewwies —'

'Nobody, of course,' said Cardew. 'D'Arcy's
been dreaming —'

'I have not been dweamin', Cardew. There was
someone heah showin' a light — lookin' wound
with a torch or somethin' — I saw it quite distinctly, and I knocked him ovah with my pillow—'

'And now he's dissolved into thin air, like jolly
old Mercury in the Aeneid?' asked Cardew.

'Weally Cardew —'

'Go to sleep and dream again!' suggested Clive.

'I wepeat that I was not dweamin'. Pewwaps he
is hidin' undah one of the beds! Look undah the
beds, deah boys.'

'Rats!' grunted Blake.

'Rot!' said Digby.

'Piffle!' said Herries.

However, they looked under the beds. Nobody was discerned under any bed. If there had been an intruder in the Fourth-form dormitory, he was gone. Only Arthur Augustus D'Arcy believed that there had been a midnight visitor at all.

'Anywhere else to look?' inquired Cardew sarcastically. 'Perhaps you fellows had better go through your pockets! He may be hiding in somebody's waistcoat pocket.'

'Ha, ha, ha!'

'Wats!' said Arthur Augustus. 'I pwesume that he dodged out of the dorm befoah the light was on. He certainly was heah —'

'Bow-wow!' said Blake. And he went back to bed. His example was followed by the other fellows. Nobody believed in Gussy's intruder: and it was clear that, if anyone had entered the dormitory at all, he was now gone.

Arthur Augustus frowned. He, at all events, was quite certain of what he had seen, and he knew that someone had been there.

'It is wathah lucky that I woke up, you fellows,' he said. 'I have no doubt that it was that funny ass Lowthah, and he would have played some twick heah if I had not spotted him.'

'Bosh!' said Blake. 'Even that ass Lowther wouldn'd be playing tricks at this time of night.'

'Hardly,' said Levison.

'Then who was it?' demanded Arthur Augustus.

'Nobody!' answered Blake.

'I wepeat —'

'Chuck it, old man.'

'I wepeat that I wepeat —'

'Is Gussy going to keep us all awake till rising-bell?' inquired Cardew. 'Are you making a night of it, D'Arcy?'

'Wats!' snapped Arthur Augustus.

And he, at last, went back to bed. Once more there was silence and slumber in the Fourth-form dormitory.

CHAPTER X

WRATHY!

'LOWTHAH, you ass —!'

'Eh!'

'You silly japin' fathead —'

'What?'

'I wegard you as a silly, japin', pwactical-jokin', footlin', fatheaded, cheeky ass!' said Arthur Augustus D'Arcy, sternly.

Monty Lowther stared. So did Manners and Tom Merry. So did Talbot of the Shell. All four were surprised by that unexpected verbal onslaught from the swell of St. Jim's.

It was morning break the next day. The four Shell fellows were in the quad, talking Soccer, when Arthur Augustus bore down on them. Arthur Augustus was not looking his accustomed genial self. His aristocratic brow was stern. His noble eye gleamed behind his eyeglass. In fact he appeared to be understudying that young man in the Alps whose brow was set and whose eye beneath flashed like a falchion from its sheath.

Something, evidently, had roused Gussy's ire. What it was, the Shell fellows had not the remotest idea. They were taken quite by surprise.

'What the jolly old thump — ?' inquired Monty Lowther.

'Anything up, Gussy?' asked Tom Merry.

'Yaas, wathah! Pewwaps you were not awah, Tom Mewwy, that that ass, that footlin' fathead, Lowthah, was out of bed last night playin' silly twicks.'

'Oh!' said Tom.

'You ass, Monty —!' said Manners.

Monty Lowther looked rather bewildered.

'Who was out of bed playing tricks?' he demanded. 'I wasn't! I never opened my eyes before rising-bell this morning.'

'Wats!' said Arthur Augustus.

'Look here —!' roared Lowther.

'I wepeat, wats!' said Arthur Augustus, firmly. 'If it was not you that came into my dorm last night, who was it? Pewwaps you can tell me, Lowthah.'

'Did anybody?' snapped Lowther.

'Yaas, wathah, and if I had not woke up, I have vewy little doubt that I should have found my twousahs sewn up again this morning,' said Arthur Augustus, sternly. 'You may wegard it as vewy funnay to sew up a fellow's twousahs, Lowthah. I do not wegard it as funnay at all. And I am vewy glad that I got you with my pillow, and I would have pillowed you wight and left if you had not got away so vewy quickly, you japin' ass.'

Tom Merry and Manners looked rather dubiously at their chum. Monty's word was as good as gold, certainly. But, on the other hand, he was a born japer, and capable of japing at any hour, even midnight's stilly hour. And it was a fact that more than once Lowther had 'larked' not wisely but too well. Neither Tom nor Manners had forgotten his bright idea the previous week of a jape in Railton's study, which they had fortunately nipped in the bud.

'Look here, Monty,' began Tom, 'If —'

Lowther gave him a glare.

'Can't you take my word?' he yapped.

'Yes, of course. But —'

'But —!' said Manners, with a shrug of the shoulders.

'I tell you I never turned out last night,' hooted Lowther. 'I was fast asleep all night: and if anybody went to that silly ass's dorm, it was not I.'

'Wats!' said Arthur Augustus, again.

'Gussy, old man,' murmured Talbot, 'Lowther knows whether he did or not, and you can take his word.'

'I wegwet that that is imposs, in the circumstances,' said Arthur Augustus. 'I know vewy well that no
othah fellow in the House would be mad ass enough
to go wound japin' aftah midnight. If it was not
Lowthah, Talbot, pewwaps you will suggest who
it might have been.'

Talbot did not answer that. In fact, if any
fellow in the School-House was harebrained
enough to play practical jokes at midnight, that
fellow was Monty Lowther, and nobody else.

'You may as well own up, Lowthah!' went on
Arthur Augustus. 'I twust that you do not suppose
that I should think of givin' you away to the
house-beak? If Wailton knew, you would get six,
and serve you jolly well wight. But Wailton is not
goin'to know.'

'There's nothing for him to know, fathead!'
howled Lowther. 'I tell you that I never turned
out last night, ass: and I was fast asleep till rising-
bell, ditherer: and if you can't take my word for
it, burbler, I'll jolly well push your silly nose
through the back of your silly head, dummy!'

'I am quite pwepared to give you a feahful
thwashin', Lowthah, if you ask for it —!'

'Steady the Buffs!' exclaimed Tom Merry. He
pushed between the two. 'Look here, Gussy, you've
made a mistake —'

'Weally, Tom Mewwy —'

'It couldn't have been Lowther, as he says it wasn't,' urged Manners.

'Weally, Mannahs —'

'Didn't you see who it was, Gussy?' asked Talbot.

'I am not a cat, Talbot. I cannot see in the dark. And the cheeky wottah dodged out of the dorm befoah a light was on. But it certainly was Lowthah because nobody else would be larkin' in the middle of the night: and I have not the slightest doubt that I have had a vewy nawwow escape of havin' my twousahs sewn up again,' said Arthur Augustus, hotly.

'Then nobody saw him?' asked Tom.

'Nobody!' answered Arthur Augustus. 'And Blake and Hewwies and Dig don't believe that there was anybody at all — in fact, all the fellows think that I dweamed it —'

'Perhaps you did!' suggested Manners.

'No perhaps about that!' snapped Monty Lowther. 'Who'd go larking in the Fourth-form dorm at midnight?'

'Only you!' said Arthur Augustus, 'And I we-gard you as a silly, weckless, japin' ass, Lowthah. And I wathah think that you may find that othah fellows can jape at midnight, if it comes to that.

Pewwpas you may find your own twousahs sewn up tomowwow mornin'!'

'You silly ass —!'

'Wats!'

With that, Arthur Augustus D'Arcy turned on his heel and walked away, with his noble nose in the air. He left the Shell fellows grinning.

'You know what to expect now, Monty, at any rate,' said Tom Merry, laughing.

Monty Lowther chuckled.

Arthur Augustus, evidently, was thinking of reprisals. Certainly it had not been his intention to alert his intended victim. He had done that without intending to do so. Unless Arthur Augustus's wrath cooled during the day, and unless slumber's chain bound him after lights-out, it was probable that the Shell dormitory would have a nocturnal visitor that night! In which case, it was equally probable that the visitor would find Monty Lowther prepared for action, and would have reason to wish that he hadn't called.

CHAPTER XI

QUITE A PUZZLE

'SKIMPOLE —!'

'Eh! Did you speak, Gore?'

'I did, you clumsy dummy.'

'My dear Gore —'

'Look what you've done!'

'But —'

'Now I'm going to punch your silly head, see?'

Talbot, coming up the Shell passage, heard the voices from his study, No. 9. His handsome face clouded in a frown.

He was on good terms with his two study-mates, Gore and Skimpole: but not uncommonly, he had to keep the peace between them. George Gore was a heavy-handed fellow; not exactly a bully, but impatient and aggressive: and Skimpole, harmless ass as he was, had many exasperating ways. Evidently, there was a spot of trouble in No. 9 now: and Talbot hastened his steps, ready to intervene and rescue Skimpole's hapless head from Gore's threatened punch.

He stepped quickly into No. 9.

Skimpole was sitting at the study table, blinking owl-like through his spectacles. On the table before him lay a massive volume that would have made any other junior's head ache to look at it. It had the cheery and attractive title of 'The Gaseous Origin of Mind and Matter'. That was the kind of mental pabulum that Skimpole enjoyed, and fancied he understood: and vastly preferred to punting a footer in the quad in morning break.

Gore was standing by the table with a French exercise in his hand. That exercise was splashed and blotted with ink, and obviously not in a state to be handed over to Monsieur Morny. On the table, an inkpot lay overturned in a pool of ink.

With the blotted exercise in his left hand, Gore was reaching across the table with his right to punch Skimpole's head, as Talbot entered. Talbot was just in time to catch his shoulder and jerk him back.

Gore glared round at him.

'Hold on,' said Talbot, pacifically. 'What's the row?'

Gore flourished the blotted exercise.

'Look at that!' he bawled. 'Think I can take that to Mossoo? I finished it after prep last night, and left it on the table — and that clumsy ass has knocked the ink over on it, and —'

'But I haven't!' protested Skimpole, blinking at him. 'The inkpot was over when I came into the study, Gore.'

'Who knocked it over, if you didn't?' bawled Gore.

'I really do not know, my dear Gore,' bleated Skimpole. 'Perhaps Talbot —'

'Not guilty,' said Talbot, smiling. 'I haven't been up to the study this morning till now. But —'

'Well, nobody else comes to the study, so it must have been that blithering chump!' exclaimed Gore. 'And I'm going to punch his silly head for spoiling my exercise. I shall have to do it over again, and I'm going to punch his head first. Let go my shoulder.'

'But I never —!' bleated Skimpole.

'Pack that up!' snapped Gore.

'Hold on, old chap,' said Talbot. 'Somebody else may have looked into the study for some reason or other —'

'Rot!' snorted Gore.

However, he unclenched his fist. Talbot was usually successful in keeping his aggressive study-mate in check. Moreover, it was clear that Talbot was not going to allow Skimpole's head to be punched: and he was twice a match for Gore if it came to hostilities. Gore snorted angrily, and left it at that.

'I assure you, my dear Gore, that I did not knock over the inkpot!' bleated Skimpole.

'Rot!' snapped Gore again. 'You're always knocking something over, you clumsy ass. Nobody else has been here. Look at my French exercise, you dummy.'

'But I assure you —'

'Oh, pack it up.'

Skimpole packed it up, and his eyes and his spectacles returned to that enthralling work, 'The Gaseous Origin of Mind and Matter'. Talbot, having established a truce, crossed the study to the book-shelf. He had come up for a book needed in third school — fortunately for Skimpole.

He put his hand to the book-shelf and then uttered an exclamation.

'Have you borrowed my Virgil, Gore?'

'I've got my own,' grunted Gore.

'Have you had it, Skimmy?'

'Eh!' Skimpole blinked up from the learned work that enthralled him. 'Did you speak to me, Talbot?'

'My Virgil isn't here,' said Talbot. 'Have you had it?'

Skimpole shook his head.

'I have not seen it, Talbot,' he answered.

Talbot turned back to the book-shelf again. That shelf accommodated books belonging to three fellows: Talbot's at one end, Gore's in the middle, and Skimpole's at the other end. Talbot, always careful with his books, had them in perfect order, and he had put his hand to the shelf to take down Virgil from its accustomed place without thinking about it.

Now, however, he looked along the row — tidy at one end, untidy in the middle and at the other end.

'Oh, here it is!' he exclaimed.

He took the volume down, with a puzzled expression on his face. That volume should have been in his own section of the shelf where he remembered clearly that he had placed it after prep the evening before. But it was not in its accustomed place. Obviously, it had been taken down from the shelf, and replaced, since he had put it there, and the person concerned had put it back in a different spot.

Talbot turned from the shelf with the book in his hand.

'You haven't had it, Gore?' he asked.

'I've said so,' grunted Gore.

'Or you, Skimmy?'

'No, my dear Talbot.'

'Then somebody has been in the study,' said Talbot. 'This book was not where I put it last evening after prep — somebody's borrowed it and put it back in the wrong place. No doubt the same chap knocked over that inkpot while he was here, Gore.'

'Oh!' said Gore. 'Sure about that book?'

'Quite!' said Talbot. 'I know exactly where I keep the book — and I've just found it among yours. Somebody's been borrowing it.'

'Oh!' said Gore again. 'Who's been rooting about our study, I'd like to know.' He scowled at his blotted exercise. 'I'd jolly well like to punch his head for giving me this to do over again.'

'Not much use punching Skimmy's as it was somebody else.'

Gore's answer to that was to grunt, and he stalked out of the study. Possibly he was glad, in the circumstances, that Talbot had interposed before Skimmy's head was punched. Skimmy certainly was!

Talbot smiled, and followed him out, leaving Skimpole to revel in 'The Gaseous Origin of Mind and Matter' till the bell called to class. In the doorway of the next study, No. 10, were three fellows, and one of them was speaking in emphatic tones. Talbot glanced along at the 'Terrible Three'. Manners seemed a little excited.

'Films are films!' he was saying, 'And they cost money! If you fellows think I can afford to buy films for my camera for you to chuck about the study and leave on the floor to be trodden on, you've got another guess coming, see!'

Talbot smiled. Manners, with his camera and his films for it, was rather like a lioness with her cubs!

'But we never touched your silly films, old man,' protested Tom Merry, 'Not a finger-tip —'

'Wouldn't touch them with a bargepole!' assured Monty Lowther.

Snort from Manners.

'They got up and stepped off the shelf, I suppose?' he suggested, sarcastically. 'If they didn't, one of you knocked them off —'

'I didn't, honest Injun!' said Tom.

'Nor I, bother you and your films,' said Lowther.

'Oh, don't talk rot,' said Manners. 'I daresay you didn't notice, being silly clumsy asses, but somebody knocked that roll of film off the bookshelf, and it was one of you silly fatheads — and if you fancy that I want my films strewn about the floor of the study to be trodden on —'

'Look here, Manners —'

'Look here, you ass —'

'Oh, rats!' said Manners, crossly. 'What's the good of arguing, when you know jolly well that nobody else could have knocked those films off the shelf —'

'I tell you —' hooted Tom Merry.

'And I tell you —!' bawled Monty Lowther.

'Oh don't talk rot —'

Talbot interposed.

'Hold on, you fellows,' he said. 'If something's been knocked over in your study —'

'No "if" about it,' snapped Manners. 'One of these clumsy asses knocked my films off the bookshelf and left them on the floor — I jolly nearly trod on them —'

'Let a fellow speak,' said Talbot. 'Something like that's happened in my study — an inkpot knocked over and a book taken down from the shelf and put back in another place. Looks as if somebody has been rooting about in your study as well as mine.'

'Oh!' said Manners, rather taken aback. 'That's jolly queer. Who the dickens would be messing about in our studies?'

Grundy of the Shell looked out of his study doorway at that point. There was a frown on his rugged face.

'Any of you been larking in my study?' he called out.

Talbot and the Terrible Three all looked round at him.

'Anything happened in your study?' asked Tom.

'Nothing much, only some ass has been mixing up my books,' answered Grundy. 'Looks as if somebody's had them down and put them back again anyhow. If you want to borrow a book, I suppose you can say so, without messing up my bookshelf.'

'But we don't want to borrow a book, and we haven't been in your study,' said Tom.

'Well somebody has!' grunted Grundy, and he turned back into his study.

'Oh!' said Manners again.

Tom Merry laughed.

'Somebody's been rooting about the studies,' he said. 'You'd better go on his trail, Manners, instead of slanging your old pals.'

'Much better!' concurred Lowther.

'Well, I thought —!' said Manners, apologetically.

'Gammon!' said Monty Lowther, 'You couldn't! Hallo, there's the bell.'

The bell for third school called the Shell fellows to the form-room. They went down, considerably puzzled: for why any fellow should have rooted in the studies and 'messed about' with the book-shelves was quite inexplicable. But they did not puzzle about it long — Latin with Mr. Linton in the Shell form-room required all their attention, and other matters were dismissed from mind.

CHAPTER XII

DONE IN THE DARK

MONTY LOWTHER grinned in the dark.

He yawned as he grinned.

It was a very late hour. In the Shell dormitory everyone but Monty Lowther was fast asleep. And Monty did not find it easy to keep awake.

In fact, he almost had to prop his eyelids open, as midnight tolled from the clock-tower. But Monty was a sticker. He was frightfully sleepy: but he was determined to keep awake, and he did.

He sat on the edge of his bed in the darkness. In his hand, resting on his knee, was a large squirt. That squirt was full of ink. And that ink was destined for the aristocratic features of Arthur Augustus D'Arcy of the Fourth Form — if that noble youth looked in after lights-out, as Monty had no doubt that he would.

Arthur Augustus quite unintentionally had given him the tip. But that was not all. During the day, Monty had kept an eye and an ear open in Gussy's direction. He was aware that Gussy had paid a visit to the matron's room, where, to that dame's considerable surprise, he had borrowed a needle and a reel of thread, for purposes unknown to Mrs. Mimms but easily guessed by Monty Lowther. There was no doubt about Gussy's dire intentions. He fully believed that the previous night Lowther had visited his dormitory with the intention of repeating his former performance — sewing up Gussy's elegant bags. He was going to give Lowther a Roland for an Oliver. Lowther, in the morning, was to find his trousers sewn up over-night: and Gussy was blissfully unconscious that Lowther knew all about it in advance.

So there was Monty Lowther, sitting up in the dark with a squirt of ink, waiting for Arthur Augustus to trickle in.

A jet of ink, landing in the middle of his features, was to be Gussy's greeting in the Shell dormitory: after which, it was improbable that he would be thinking further of sewing up any fellow's trousers.

That cheery jest on Gussy was worth sitting up for, in the opinion of the funny man of the Shell, and he sat up.

Every now and then he nodded and had to pull himself together. His eyelids drooped in spite of himself. And, as midnight approached, he began to wonder whether, after all, D'Arcy had gone to sleep and forgotten all about it — in which case, he had his nocturnal vigil for nothing.

That was a rather discouraging thought: and, as midnight boomed, Monty began rather to wish that he had turned in with the other fellows. But he was a sticker, and he stuck.

Suddenly, he gave a little start.

There was a faint sound from the direction of the door.

Lowther's eyes gleamed as he caught it.

It was a relief to him. It would have been exceedingly exasperating to have sat up to such an hour for nothing. But it was all right now — Gussy was coming at last. He had left it very late: but he was coming! Had Lowther been asleep in bed, as a surreptitious visitor to the dormitory would have expected every fellow there to be, he would not have heard the faint sound of the door opening softly and stealthily. As it was, he heard it quite distinctly.

He rose silently from the bed on which he sat. With noiseless footsteps, he stepped towards the opening door.

A chill draught from the passage showed that it was open, though he could see nothing in the darkness.

He stood still, his head bent a little, listening intently. The squirt was full of ink: but there was only one shot in the locker, so to speak: and he was taking no chance of missing his target in the dark.

The faintest of stealthy footfalls told where the unseen intruder was. He caught a sound of suppressed breathing. Then came a sudden glimmer of light, as a little electric torch was switched on. Lowther did not need to risk a shot in the dark! He could not see the intruder behind the light: but the light itself was a perfect guide to his aim.

Swisssssh!

'Oooooogh!' came a startled, gurgling gasp.

The light went out instantly.

In the darkness, there was a sound of horrible gurgling. It sounded as if some of the ink had gone into a mouth.

'Yrrrrrrrgh!'

'Ha, ha, ha!' yelled Monty Lowther.

'Gurrrrrgggggh!'

'Ha, ha, ha! Got him!' trilled Lowther.

'Wurrrrggggh!'

'Like it, Gussy? Ha, ha, ha!'

There was hurried panting and gurgling. It was accompanied by the sound of hurried feet. The intruder, smothered and dripping with ink, gurglink ink, was in hasty retreat.

'Ha, ha, ha! Good-night, Gussy!' chortled Lowther.

The door closed with a snap.

'Ha, ha, ha!'

'Is that you, Lowther, you ass?' came from Tom Merry's bed. He sat up, peering in the dark. Lowther's yell of laughter had awakened half the Shell.

'What on earth's happening?' exclaimed Talbot.

'That fathead Lowther —!' came from Manners.

'Ha, ha, ha!' trilled Lowther. 'It was Gussy — good old Gussy — he came here to sew up my trousers, and I got him with my squirt! I fancy he will want some washing before he goes back to bed. Ha, ha, ha!'

Tom Merry laughed.

'Poor old Gussy!' he said. 'The innocent old lamb doesn't know that he tipped you about what he was going to do.'

'Ha, ha, ha!'

'Gussy all over!' said Talbot, laughing.

'Sure you got him, in the dark?' asked Tom.

'He turned on a light — of course, he had to have a light to sew up a fellow's trousers!' chuckled Lowther. 'He didn't dream that any fellow here was awake — he wouldn't! I fancy he swallowed some of the ink — it sounded like it! Ha, ha, ha!'

Monty Lowther laughed loud and long. He was

tired, and he was sleepy: but his midnight vigil had been a complete success! In those very moments, he had no doubt, the unfortunate swell of St. Jim's was frantically washing off ink in the Fourth-form dormitory. It was quite an amusing mental picture. Lowther chuckled and chuckled.

He went back to bed, at last, in a very cheery mood. After the other fellows had gone to sleep again, there were chuckles from Monty Lowther's bed. But once his eyes closed, they remained closed as if glued, and did not reopen till the rising-bell was ringing in the misty winter morning. After so late a vigil, he slept very soundly; and if he dreamed, he certainly did not dream that it was not Arthur Augustus D'Arcy, the ornament of the Fourth Form, who had been the recipient of that squirt-full of ink in the dark!

CHAPTER XIII

TROUBLESOME TROUSERS

'WAKE up!'
   'Yaw-aw-aw-aw!'
   'Turn out, fathead!'
   'Yaw-aw-aw-aw!'
   'Bell's stopping.'
   'Yaw-aw-aw!'

Monty Lowther, as a rule, was one of the first out of bed in the Shell dormitory in the School House. He was wont to leap cheerily from it, even on a cold wintry morning.

But on this particular morning, Monty was not feeling his usual buoyant self. Buoyancy in the morning requires a good night's rest over-night. And Monty had sat up till after midnight.

True, he had slept very soundly when, at last, he did get to bed. But he had lost some hours of sleep: and he was feeling the effect of that loss when the rising-bell clanged. Instead of being one of the first out of bed, he was last on the list: and was still in bed when other fellows were ready to go down.

Tom Merry called him: Manners called: Talbot called him in turn: only sleepy yawns answered. For once, Lowther was reluctant to rise: and he was staying in bed till the latest possible moment.

The rising-bell ceased to clang. Tom Merry and Talbot and Kangaroo, and other fellows who like a shower even on a winter's morning, took their towels and scuttled up the passage to the bath: other fellows, less hardy, splashed soap and water in the dormitory. Heedless of all, Monty Lowther closed his eyes on his pillow, and snatched an extra few minutes. He would have given a great deal for an extra hour in bed that morning.

But that was not to be. His eyes reopened as he felt a shake, and he blinked up at Tom Merry, fresh as paint from cold water.

'Yaw-aw-aw!' yawned Monty.

'Get out, fathead.'

'Another minute or two —'

'You'll be late for prayers, ass. Up with you.'

'Oh, dear!' mumbled Lowther. 'I'm jolly sleepy.'

'I'll give you something for that!' said Tom, cheerily, and he dabbed a wet sponge on Lowther's face — which quite effectually made him wide-awake on the spot. He bounded.

'Keep that sponge away, you silly ass!' he howled.

'Getting up?' asked Tom.

'Yes, blow you.'

Lowther rolled out of bed at last. Some of the Shell fellows were going down. A voice floating in from the passage told that some of the Fourth were already out of their dormitory. The dulcet tones of Arthur Augustus D'Arcy, of that form, were audible.

'Glyn, old chap, is Lowthah up yet?'

'Not yet — he's sleepy this morning.'

'Ha, ha, ha!'

'What's the joke, D'Arcy?'

'Lowthah, deah boy! Ha, ha, ha!'

Which was rather mystifying to the fellows in the Shell dormitory, who heard. Monty Lowther was quite puzzled.

'That's Gussy,' he said. 'What's he sniggering about this morning? Does he like being squirted with ink in the middle of the night?'

'Never mind Gussy,' said Tom. 'Get going you ass — we'll wait for you, but bundle into your clobber, for goodness' sake — we can't be late.'

Monty Lowther proceeded to 'bundle'. But, as he drew his trousers on, there was a sudden startled howl from him.

'Oh, crumbs! What silly ass has done this?'

'What — ?'

'Which — ?'

'My bags!' yelled Lowther.

He had dragged on his trousers in a hurry. But his feet did not emerge therefrom. They seemed to be bottled up in the legs of the trousers.

Tom Merry and Manners stared. The other fellows had gone down by this time, but they were waiting impatiently — for their chum. Lowther, sitting on the edge of his bed, dragged furiously at his trousers — but those garments refused to come up over his feet.

'What the dickens — ?' exclaimed Tom Merry.

'Sewn up!' yelled Lowther.

'Wh-a-a-t?'

'Look!'

'Oh, my hat!'

Lowther kicked off the trousers and held them up. Manners and Tom Merry blinked at them. Some surreptitious hand had been at work in the hours of darkness. Both the legs of the trousers were sewn up at the ends: and plenty of stitches had been put in.

'Ha, ha, ha!' yelled Tom and Manners.

Lowther gave them an almost ferocious glare.

'Think it's funny?' he bawled.

Tom Merry chuckled.

You thought it funny when you sewed up D'Arcy's bags one night,' he said. 'But I suppose a lot depends on whose bags are sewn up.'

'What silly chump did this?' howled Lowther, who evidently did not think it at all funny for his own 'bags' to be sewn up, funny as it had seemed in the case of Arthur Augustus D'Arcy. 'By gum, I'll punch his silly head —'

'Never mind his silly head now, whoever he was,' said Tom, laughing. 'Get into them somehow — we shall be late —'

'By gum, I-I-I'll —,' gasped Lowther.

'Hurry up!' said Manners.

Lowther wrenched at the 'bags'. But they had been sewn up well and truly, and he wrenched in vain. He breathed wrath and vengeance as he wrenched. He had not a moment to spare: and those bags were an insoluble problem. Time and patience were required: and Lowther had neither available.

He hurled the garments across the dormitory at last and ran to his box. There he hurriedly sorted out his Sunday 'bags'. Tom Merry and Manners, laughing, waited while he plunged into them.

An eyeglass gleamed in at the open doorway.

'Good-mornin' you fellows!' said Arthur Augustus D'Arcy, cheerily. 'Findin' any twouble with your clobbah, Lowthah?'

Monty Lowther jumped.

'You!' he roared.

'Gussy!' exclaimed Tom Merry and Manners together. It dawned on all three who was responsible for the sewing-up of those bags.

Arthur Augustus chuckled.

'One good turn deserved anothah!' he said. 'It's a Woland for an Olivah. Ha, ha, ha!'

'You!' bawled Lowther.

'Yaas, wathah!' chuckled Arthur Augustus. 'You weally might have guessed that you would get somethin' back for playin' twicks in my dorm, Lowthah — but you were fast asleep when I came in. I was wathah late, it is twue, as I fell asleep when we went to bed and did not wake up till vewy late, long aftah midnight, but I turned out all the same —'

'You burbling image, it was midnight when you came here —' howled Lowther. 'I thought one squirt of ink would be enough for you —'

'Eh!'

'If I'd known you'd come back after I squirted you, I'd have had another lot ready —'

Arthur Augustus looked bewildered.

'I fail to undahstand you, Lowthah,' he answered.

*Both the legs of the trousers had been sewn up
at the ends*

'You were fast asleep when I came here, and you certainly did not squirt me with ink!'

'Oh, don't be an ass! I was up and watching for you, and got you full in your silly mug with a squirt of ink —'

'You have been dweamin', Lowthah! I wepeat that you were fast asleep when I came heah about one in the mornin' —'

'Oh, suffering cats!' exclaimed Tom Merry. 'Wasn't it Gussy you got with that squirt, Monty?'

'Of course it was!' hooted Lowther. 'Who else?'

'Bai Jove! Did you weally squirt somebody with ink?' asked Arthur Augustus. 'Who was it?'

'You!' yelled Lowther.

Arthur Augustus shook his head.

'If you got anybody with a squirt, it certainly was not I,' he said. 'I found the whole dorm fast asleep at one in the mornin' and I was a quartah of an hour sewin' up your bags and nobody woke up — and you were as fast asleep as Wip van Winkle.' Arthur Augustus chuckled. 'Pewwaps you will think twice about larkin' in anothah fellow's dormitory aftah this, Lowthah — you are liable to get a Woland for an Olivah! Ha, ha, ha!'

Lowther clutched up a pillow.

Arthur Augustus stepped rather hastily back

from the doorway in time. He was heard to laugh as he went down the passage.

Lowther dropped the pillow.

'What the dickens dees that mean?' he asked. 'If it wasn't D'Arcy, who got the ink —'

'It wasn't,' said Tom, laughing. 'You got somebody about midnight — and it was a good bit later, according to Gussy, that he came here. But who the dickens it could have been —'

'I was sure it was D'Arcy, of course. Who else would come here, except that silly ass on a rag?'

'Goodness knows,' said Manners. 'But it wasn't D'Arcy. Somebody else was pottering about last night, and you got him — and then went to bed and left the coast clear for Gussy —'

'But who?' gasped Lowther. He realised that it was not, after all, Arthur Augustus who had captured that squirt-full of ink in the dark. But who else it could have been was a mystery.

'Some chap larking —!' said Tom. 'Goodness knows who —'

'There's the bell,' said Manners.

'Come on, Monty.'

It was quite a mystery: but it had to be left unsolved. The chums of the Shell scuttled down the passage and down the stairs, Lowther fastening final buttons as he rushed.

CHAPTER XIV

MYSTERIOUS

'LOWTHAH —'
  'Fathead!'
  'Weally, Lowthah —'
  'Ass!'
  'I have just looked in —'
  'Now look out again!'
  'I was goin' to say —'
  'Rats!'
Tom Merry laughed: Manners chuckled, and Talbot smiled. They seemed rather amused by that colloquy.

Four Shell fellows, in No. 10. study, were at tea when Arthur Augustus D'Arcy looked in. Over tea, they were discussing the curious episode of the night before in their dormitory. Three of the four gave Gussy quite amicable glances as his eyeglass gleamed into the study: but Monty Lowther bestowed a glare upon him. Monty, apparently, had not yet forgotten those troublesome trousers of the morning. Like many humorists, Monty did not wholly enjoy a joke at his own expense. Gussy's struggles with sewn-up bags were amusing: his own, seemingly, were not!

'I insist upon speakin'!' said Arthur Augustus, warmly. 'I have looked in to say that I appeah to have made a mistake, Lowthah —'

'Do you ever make anything else, ass?'

'Fwom what has twanspired,' continued Arthur Augustus, unheeding, 'it appeahs that some unknown person has been wootin' about the dormitowies aftah lights-out. You squirted ink ovah him last night, fancyin' that it was I —'

'Wish it had been!'

'Wats! It was not I,' said Arthur Augustus. 'I came latah, aftah you had gone back to bed. It was somebody else, goodness knows who. In the circumstances, Lowthah, I must admit that pwobably it was not you who butted into my dorm the night befoah, but pwobably the same pwowlah. I wegwet that I did not take your word on the subject. But weally, Lowthah, you are such a funnay ass, what did you expect a fellow to think?'

'I didn't expect you to think at all,' answered Lowther.

'Weally, you cheekay ass —'

'Shut the door after you.'

'I wegwet that I did not accept your assuwance

on the subject,' said Arthur Augustus, 'but I do
not wegwet that I sewed up your twousahs, Lowthah. You played that twick on me once, and if
your own twicks come home to woost, you have
no kick comin'. And I will say furthah — yawooh!'
roared Arthur Augustus, suddenly, as a banana-
skin whizzed through the air, and landed on his
noble nose, and then dropped at his feet.

'Ha, ha, ha!'

'Oh, cwikey!' Arthur Augustus rubbed his nose.
'Lowthah, you wuffian —'

'Ha, ha, ha!'

'Bai Jove!' Arthur Augustus, in great wrath,
made a rush at Monty Lowther.

It was like Gussy to tread on the banana-skin as
he rushed.

That banana-skin was slippery: and Gussy
slipped. He did not reach Lowther on his feet: he
reached him on his hands and knees. There was
a howl of laughter in No. 10 study as the swell
of St. Jim's nose-dived.

'Oh!' gasped Arthur Augustus, dizzily.

'Ha, ha, ha!'

'Do that again, Gussy!'

'Ha, ha, ha!'

Arthur Augustus scrambled up, red with wrath.
Monty Lowther jumped up, and picked up the

teapot from the table. Only a swift backward jump saved the swell of St. Jim's from a stream of hot tea.

'Lowthah, you wottah — keep that teapot away,' yelled Arthur Augustus, with another backward jump, as Monty followed him up.

'Ha, ha, ha!'

Bang! Arthur Augustus, with another backward jump into the passage, closed the study door with a bang that woke every echo in the Shell studies. He departed in wrath, and the Shell fellows, grinning, resumed their tea; and their discussion of the mysterious episode of the night.

'It's a queer business,' said Tom Merry. 'I've been trying to puzzle it out, but I just can't guess who it was that barged into the dorm last night.'

'Jolly queer,' said Manners. 'I've asked fellows right and left, but can't hear of any chap who got inked.'

'That ink must have taken a lot of washing off,' said Lowther, with a nod. 'Whoever he was, he got it fair and square, but nobody seems to have seen any fellow washing off ink.'

Talbot nodded, thoughtfully.

'We know it wasn't a Shell fellow,' he said, 'and it can't have been a Fourth-form man — some of them would know. Can't have been some cheeky fag from the Third Form, I suppose?'

'Hardly,' said Tom. 'I should think it was
a House rag from Figgins and Co. over the way:
but New House men couldn't have done it, after
lights-out. But if it's some School House man
playing the giddy ass, who the dickens is he, and
what is he doing it for?'

'Must be up to something,' said Manners. 'Somebody rooting about the studies and dormitories after
lights-out, that's clear. He barged into our dorm last
night, and into the Fourth-form dorm the night
before. Gussy thought it was Lowther and Lowther
thought it was Gussy: but it wasn't either. But it
was the same chap, there's no doubt, who messed
about in the studies — meddling with the books
on the shelves. Not only ours, and Talbot's and
Grundy's — I heard Glyn saying that somebody
had moved his microscope and some Fourth-form
chaps have been saying that things have been
messed about in their studies. Somebody's prowling
about at night — but who — and why?'

Tom Merry shook his head.

'I give up!' he said.

'It's not some funny ass like Monty, playing
practical jokes,' went on Manners. 'Nothing's been
damaged, except Gore's French paper, and that
looks as if the inkpot was knocked over by accident
while somebody was groping about. But what on

earth is the chap after? Looks as if he's looking for something — but what?'

'What do you think, Talbot?' asked Tom. Tom had great faith in the sagacity of the junior whose experience had been so unlike that of other St. Jim's fellows. In many ways, Talbot was older than his years.

But Talbot could only shake his head. He was as puzzled as the Terrible Three.

'I can't make it out at all,' he confessed. 'It's plain that some fellow prowls about at night: but who, and why, I can't begin to guess. But one thing's pretty clear — he's up to no good. A fellow doesn't steal about in the middle of the night with any good motive. He ought to be stopped.'

'Yes, rather,' said Tom. 'If this goes on, it will get to the house-beak, with so much talk on the subject, and Railton will take it up and there will be a row. But what can we do?'

'Nothing — unless somebody stays up to watch for him.'

'Um!' said Manners.

'Um!' said Tom, like an echo.

'Um!' added Monty Lowther. 'I had enough last night! It was more than a bit parky, I can tell you.'

Evidently the idea of sitting up late on a winter's night did not seem attractive.

Talbot smiled, and did not repeat his suggestion. But when tea was over, and Manners and Lowther went down, he lingered in the study to speak to Tom. His face was very thoughtful.

'Look here, Tom,' he said quietly. 'This is a jolly queer matter, and it ought to be cleared up. I don't see any way except some fellow keeping watch and catching the prowler, whoever he is, and putting a stop to it. Do you?'

'No!' said Tom. 'But —'

'I shall take it on,' said Talbot. He smiled faintly, the colour coming into his cheeks as he spoke. 'It's easier for me than for any other fellow, Tom — I've had experience of night prowling, as you know —'

'Talbot!' breathed Tom.

'It's true, Tom — in the old days, the Toff was very often awake while others slept!' said Talbot. 'It's nothing to me to be alert in the dark, Tom. Leave it to me: and if the prowler prowls again tonight, it will be his last prowl.'

'I'll stay up with you,' said Tom.

'No need, old chap! Leave it to me.'

And it was agreed that it should be left to Talbot. And at a late hour that night, Talbot slipped quietly from his bed and dressed in the dark — little dreaming what the outcome was to be!

CHAPTER XV

DARK DOUBTS

MR. RAILTON frowned.

Seldom had the kind, good-tempered face of the School House master worn so dark a look.

It was midnight.

At that hour the house-master was, as a rule, as deep in slumber as any fellow in the School House. But matters were not as usual now. Railton was sitting up late; and as the stroke of midnight came from the clock-tower, he switched off the light in his study.

But he was not thinking of bed.

Tom Merry had remarked in No. 10 that, if the 'prowling' went on, it would get to the house-master. As a matter of fact, it had already reached the ears of Victor Railton. Fifty fellows, at least, had been discussing it during the day: the mysterious prowler who had been inked in the Shell dormitory was a general topic. Precisely what had occurred Railton did not know: and he had asked no questions: but he did know that some person unknown was prowling in the House at night: dozens of remarks that floated to his ears left him in no doubt about that. And his immediate decision was to put 'paid' to that mysterious prowler without delay. Once his grasp had closed on the prowler's collar, 'six' of the very best would warn him off such reckless nocturnal activities.

It was for that reason that Mr. Railton was up so late that night. It was a repugnant task: he did not like the idea of keeping watch. But that, as Talbot had told his friends, was the only way of catching the prowler: little dreaming that the same idea was in his house-master's mind.

Having put out his light, Mr. Railton opened his study door.

The House was in darkness.

He stepped into the corridor without a sound, in soft slippers. He had an electric torch in his pocket: but he did not need a light: every inch of the School House was familiar to him.

Silently, he passed up the big staircase.

On the study landing, he paused and listened. But there was no sound in the stillness of the night. He moved on, silently, to the dormitory staircase. Above was another landing, which gave access to the dormitories. It was on that landing that Railton

intended to station himself, and wait in the dark
for a sign of the prowler.

He made no sound as he mounted the stairs.
A flitting spectre could not have been more silent.
If the prowler was about, there was to be no sound
to give him alarm — till he was caught!

He reached the dormitory landing.

The faintest of faint glimmers came from high
windows. The night was dark. All was shadowy
gloom about him.

But suddenly he stopped dead, almost ceasing to
breathe. In the silence and darkness, it seemed to
him that he heard a breath. And it rushed into his
mind that he was not alone on the dark landing.

His lips set hard.

The prowler was there — he had almost walked
into him. He was sure of it. Someone was on that
landing in the dark — invisible in the blackness,
but quite near him.

Motionless, silent, he listened. Then, with
a sudden plunge forward, he groped in the dark
and his outstretched hand touched an unseen figure.
He heard a startled gasp.

His grasp closed on that unseen figure: while,
with his other hand, he groped in his pocket for his
torch.

But, to his surprise, for he had not expected

resistance, he was grasped in his turn, in a pair
of strong hands. But his own grasp did not relax.

His hand came out of his pocket, with the torch
in it, and he flashed on the light.

It gleamed full on a familiar face.

Railton almost staggered, in his surprise.

'Talbot!' he gasped.

'Mr. Railton!' stuttered Talbot.

As he realised who it was that he had grasped in
the dark, Talbot released his grip instantly. He stood
blinking in the light that streamed on his face.

'Talbot!' repeated Railton. 'You!'

'I-I-!' stammered Talbot.

'You!'

'I-I didn't know it was you, sir — I wouldn't
have touched you — I couldn't see in the dark —'

'What are you doing out of your dormitory,
Talbot?' In Mr. Railton's face, astonishment was
giving way to grim anger and suspicion. In all the
School House, Talbot of the Shell was probably
the last person he would have thought of in connection with the 'prowler'. But it was Talbot of
the Shell that he had caught in the dark on the
dormitory landing.

'I-I-I can explain, sir —!' stammered Talbot.
He was utterly dismayed and disconcerted by this
unexpected encounter.

'You will have to explain!' said Mr. Railton, sternly. 'I find you, Talbot, fully dressed, out of your dormitory at midnight. I —'

'Please let me explain, sir!' panted Talbot. 'I was keeping watch — I know, sir, that it is against the rules for any fellow to leave his dormitory after light-out, but —'

'Keeping watch?' repeated Mr. Railton. 'What do you mean?'

'You wouldn't know, sir, but some fellow, nobody knows who, has been prowling the House at night —'

'Not you!' said Mr. Railton, grimly.

Talbot started.

'I!' he exclaimed.

'I had become aware, Talbot, of the prowling you speak of,' said the house-master, sternly. 'It is for that reason that I am here now.'

'Oh!' gasped Talbot.

'And it is you that I have caught!' said Mr. Railton.

Talbot's face crimsoned.

'Oh sir! You can't suppose — you couldn't believe — if you want proof, if you can't take my word, Tom Merry knows that I was to stay up and keep watch tonight — he will tell you —'

Keeping the light on his face, the house-master

scanned him long and hard. A few days ago he
had been displeased with Talbot, in the affair of
D'Arcy's lines. But that was a trifle — this was
not a trifle. He had expected, if he caught the
prowler, to catch some unthinking, foolish practical-
joker. But it was Talbot — it was the 'Toff' of other
days that he had caught. It was the one-time
member of Hookey Walker's gang who was out
of bed, out of his dormitory, at midnight! If the
Toff, the one-time boy-cracksman of Angel Alley,
was the prowler, why? Darker and darker grew the
house-master's brow. No other fellow in the School
House, so far as Railton could surmise, had any
object, could have any object, in 'prowling' at
night. But the Toff, if he had slid back into old
lawless ways, might have an object!

Talbot's face was crimson: but the crimson
faded leaving him deadly pale, as he read the
thought in his house-master's mind — easily to
be read in his face.

He caught his breath.

'Mr. Railton!' His voice came unsteadily. 'If
you think — if you suspect — if you do not trust
me —' His voice cracked.

The house-master's stern face relaxed a little.

'I have trusted you, Talbot!' he said. 'I know
all your story and I have trusted you in spite of

it: and so far I have no reason to lose my faith in you. But now —' He paused a moment. 'From talk that has reached me, I know that some person has been prowling the House at night. I can imagine no reason why anyone should do so, except some utterly unthinking and irresponsible practical-joker, unless —'

'Unless —!' breathed Talbot, almost inaudibly.

'Unless with a dishonest motive,' said M. Railton. 'Unless as a thief in the night, Talbot.'

Talbot shuddered.

'If, as you say, you left your dormitory tonight to watch for the prowler, you acted with injudicious rashness,' said the house-master. 'You, more than any other boy at this school, should be careful to avoid any possibility of misunderstanding or misconception. But —' he paused again, and this time the pause was longer.

He had trusted the boy. He believed in him, and he had respected him for the strength of mind with which he had thrown over his old life, and set his feet on a new path. And, suspicious as were the circumstances, now he felt that he trusted him still.

He spoke at last.

'It was not you, Talbot, who prowled the House, and caused so much exceitment among the juniors?'

'No, sir!'

'You do not know who it was?'

'I cannot guess — but I hoped to catch him, and put a stop to it. When we collided in the dark, I thought I had caught him — as you did, sir — that was why I grasped hold —'

'I understand that!'

'I know that I have broken a rule of the House in leaving my dormitory, sir — but that is all.' Talbot's voice was steadier. 'I did not know that you knew anything about it — I should have left it to you if I had known. If you cannot take my word, sir —'

'I do take your word, Talbot!' said Mr. Railton. 'I had a great shock, finding you here — but I do take your word.'

'Thank you sir!' said Talbot, in a low voice.

'You may return to your dormitory, and nothing more will be said about this,' said the house-master. 'I shall trust you, Talbot, as I have trusted you hitherto: but let there be no more of this! The matter is in my hands. Go to bed at once.'

'Yes, sir!' said Talbot, quietly.

He went without another word. The house-master, with a thoughtful brow, watched him as he went: and then shut off his light. In the darkness, his face was thoughtful and troubled. He had trusted Talbot — and he trusted him still: yet the 'Toff'

might have a motive for night-prowling and what
other fellow in the School House had? But he
drove that dark doubt resolutely from his mind.

For a whole weary hour, after Talbot had gone
back to his dormitory, Mr. Railton remained on
the landing, silent and wary. But there was no sign
or sound of a 'prowler' and at last he gave it up
and went to bed. And on the following night, when
he repeated his vigil, the result was the same. The
unknown and mysterious prowler of the School
House had ceased to prowl!

CHAPTER XVI

THE RAGGER RAGGED

ARTHUR AUGUSTUS D'ARCY grinned.

He was amused.

Arthur Augustus was in No. 10 study in the
Shell: where, really, no Fourth-form fellow had
any business to be, in the absence of the proprietors.
But Arthur Augustus, as it happened, had business
there — business that could only be carried on in
the absence of those proprietors.

He was standing before the study arm-chair. In
one of his aristocratic hands was a large bottle of
gum. In the other was a bottle of ink. He was
pouring from both bottles — into the seat of the
arm-chair.

He grinned as he poured.

'Bai Jove!' murmured Arthur Augustus. 'This
sort of thing is wathah below a fellow's dignity:
but if a fellow plays twicks in anothah fellow's
study, he must weally expect his twicks to come
home to woost. It did not seem funnay to me to
find gum in my toppah — but pewwaps Lowthah

will think it funnay to sit down in it — he is such a funnay ass!'

And Arthur Augustus chuckled.

Gussy, generally the most placable of fellows, was on the war-path. Gum in his topper had roused his ire. Hence his surreptitious visit to No. 10 study, while Tom Merry and Manners and Lowther were down in the day-room. Whoever sat in that gummy and inky arm-chair would, no doubt, realise that japing with gum was not a paying proposition. Gussy hoped that it would be Monty Lowther who sat in it. Anyhow, it would be one of the Terrible Three: and a warning to that study that disrespectful hands were not to be laid on a fellow's topper with impunity.

The ink ran out and Gussy dropped the bottle under the table. The gum exuded more slowly. But it all oozed out at last. The seat of the arm-chair swam in a mixture of gum and ink. Then the gum bottle joined the ink-bottle under the table. Arthur Augustus, his deadly work done, turned to the door.

Then he gave a sudden jump.

'Oh, cwikey!' he breathed.

There were footsteps and voices in the passage outside. The Terrible Three were coming up to their study.

'Oh, bai Jove!'

It was a dismaying moment. What would happen if the Shell fellows caught him in their study, with the arm-chair in its present state, Arthur Augustus could guess. It would undoubtedly be something unpleasant.

For a moment he stood undecided. Then he backed rapidly behind the door, so that it would conceal him when it opened. There was a chance, at least, if the Shell fellows did not see him when they came in, of making a sudden rush and escaping. It was Gussy's only chance.

He backed close to the wall as the door opened. Tom Merry and Manners and Lowther came into the study. If they had closed the door, they must have seen Arthur Augustus immediately. But, for the moment, they did not close the door. Monty Lowther was speaking as they came in.

'Wet blankets —!' he was saying.

'Give us a rest!' sighed Tom Merry.

'Spoiling a jolly good jape on the house-beak—'

'We've heard that one!' said Manners.

Snort, from Monty Lowther.

'Chance of a lifetime!' he said. 'Think Railton's likely to drop his key about the house again.'

'Not likely,' agreed Tom Merry.

'It was just lucky my picking it up on the stairs— the key of his money-drawer. Fancy his face if he'd found his bank-notes missing, and the drawer still locked!'

'I suppose it's no use talking sense to you, Monty,' said Tom Merry. 'You can't understand anything beyond a joke. But no fellow who wasn't a born idiot would think of playing tricks with money.'

'Like to be suspected of pinching it?' asked Manners.

'Oh, don't be an ass!' snapped Lowther. 'Railton would have found it in his study sooner or later — I was only going to hide the bank-notes and give him a hunt for them. Just a jest on him —'

'Bai Jove!' murmured Arthur Augustus, as he heard that, behind the door, 'Of all the potty, japin' asses —' he murmured inaudibly.

'No end of a lark on Railton!' went on Lowther. 'But you fellows are too solemn to live! You can't see a joke.'

'Not that sort!' said Manners.

'Not at all,' said Tom, 'and thank goodness you're never likely to get hold of Railton's key again, you dangerous lunatic.'

'Wet blankets!' snorted Monty Lowther. 'If Railton drops that key again and I jolly well get hold of it, I'll jolly well carry on, and tell you fellows about it afterwards, and —'

'It's not likely to happen,' said Tom Merry, laughing, 'But if it did, we'd jolly well scalp you, Monty. Keep your japing for junior studies — Gussy's toppers in No. 6 — and leave house-beaks alone. And — Oh, my hat! What's that?'

Tom Merry broke off, with a sudden jump, as the study-door suddenly flew out from the wall, apparently of its own volition.

For a split second, it was quite amazing. But the mystery was revealed the next moment, as an elegant figure, hitherto concealed behind the door, made a leap for the doorway.

Another split second, and Arthur Augustus would have been through the doorway and speeding down the passage. But Monty Lowther interposed a foot just in time.

'Yawoooooh!' roared Arthur Augustus, as he stumbled over the foot and measured his length in the doorway.

'Gussy —!' exclaimed Tom Merry.

'What the dickens —!' exclaimed Manners.

'Oh, cwikey! Oh, bai Jove!' Arthur Augustus struggled dizzily up. But there was no escape for Gussy now. Three Shell fellows gathered round him and barged him further into the study.

'Now, what's this game?' demanded Tom Merry.

'Weally, Tom Mewwy —'

'What have you been up to in our study?'
demanded Manners. 'If you've been messing about
with my camera —'

'Bothah your camewah —'

'Oh, my hat!' yelled Monty Lowther. 'Look!'
He pointed to the arm-chair, the seat of which
glistened with gum and ink.

Tom Merry and Manners gazed at it. Then they
gazed at Arthur Augustus D'Arcy. Their gaze was
expressive.

'You footling fathead —!' exclaimed Tom.

'You benighted chump —!' said Manners.

'Japing in our study!' exclaimed Monty Lowther.
'That ass! Why, you dithering duffer —'

'I did not intend to let you discovah me heah,'
said Arthur Augustus. 'I was goin' to leave you
to wowwy it out, just as you did when you gummed
my toppah, Lowthah. If you gum a fellow's toppah,
Lowthah, you must weally expect somethin' in
weturn. I .wathah considahed that it might be a
warnin' to you when your japin' came home to
woost. I only wegwet that nobody will sit in that
gummy arm-chair now!'

Monty Lowther chuckled.

'Somebody will!' he said.

'What-ho!' chuckled Tom Merry.

'Hear, hear!' grinned Manners.

And the three Shell fellows grasped Arthur Augustus D'Arcy on all sides, and propelled him backwards towards the gummy, inky arm-chair. There was a yell of alarm from the swell of St. Jim's.

'Bai Jove! Stoppit! Welease me! I wefuse to sit in that arm-chair! It will wuin my twousahs —'

'Ha, ha, ha!'

'Welease me, you wottahs!' shrieked Arthur Augustus. He struggled frantically, as he was propelled backwards.

But his struggles were unavailing. Back he went, and back, till the back of his noble knees contacted the chair. There he made a final frantic resistance, and for a moment or two maintained his balance. But three pairs of hands shoved, and shoved hard — and he sat down.

Plump! Squelch!

'Oh, cwikey!'

Arthur Augustus sat suddenly and hard in the arm-chair. Ink and gum squelched round him. Then he was released. He bounded up as if the arm-chair had been red hot. He bolted for the door. He left a trail of dripping gum and ink behind him as he bolted. The most elegant trousers at St. Jim's dripped inky gum.

'Ha, ha, ha!' yelled Tom Merry and Co.

'Gwooooogh!' gasped Arthur Augustus.

'Ha, ha, ha!'

Oh, cwumbs! My twousahs —'

'Ha, ha, ha!'

Arthur Augustus disappeared, a yell of laughter following him as he went. Arthur Augustus did not heed it. What he wanted just then, more than anything else, was a change of trousers: and he hurried off in search of the same: leaving the chums of the Shell yelling.

CHAPTER XVII

UNDER THE SHADOW

'OH! Heah you are, deah boy.'

Arthur Augustus D'Arcy made that remark, as he looked into No. 9 study in the Shell a few days later.

It was addressed to Talbot.

The Shell fellow was sitting on the edge of the study table, his hands driven deep into his pockets, his brow darkly clouded. If he heard the voice in the doorway he did not heed it. He did not look round, or answer: and Arthur Augustus raised his eyebrows in surprise.

'Talbot, deah boy!' he proceeded.

Still no answer.

'I twust, Talbot, that you have not suddenly become deaf!' said Arthur Augustus, with mild sarcasm.

Talbot heeded at last. He made an irritable movement, and glanced round impatiently at the swell of St. Jim's.

'Don't bother!' he said.

'Weally, Talbot —'

'Run away and play, and shut that door.'

'Bai Jove! I looked in —'

'I can see that! Now look out again.'

Arthur Augustus's brow knitted in a frown.

It was unusual, very unusual, for Talbot of the Shell to be impatient and snappish. He seemed to be both now. It reminded Arthur Augustus of that evening in Wayland Lane. But what was the matter with Talbot now he could not guess. It was a fine, clear afternoon: a half-holiday: and Soccer was on: which surely was enough to make any fellow merry and bright. But Talbot certainly looked neither merry nor bright. Having snapped at Arthur Augustus, he turned his back to him again.

'I am sowwy to bore you, Talbot —!' said Arthur Augustus, more sarcastic than before, 'But I looked in to say —'

'Oh, leave me alone.'

Arthur Augustus breathed hard and he breathed deep. He did not speak again. He drew the door shut with a snap, and walked away: leaving the Shell fellow to his own gloomy reflections whatever they were.

With a frown on his noble brow, the swell of St.

Jim's went down to the changing-room. There was a crowd of juniors there, most of them in the process of changing for football.

Tom Merry called across to Arthur Augustus, as he came in.

'Where's Talbot, D'Arcy?'

'In his study, Tom Mewwy.'

'Well, isn't he coming down?' asked Tom, puzzled.

'I am quite unawah of his intentions,' answered Arthur Augustus, stiffly, 'I am not intewested in him at all.'

Tom stared. .

'What's biting you now?' he asked.

'I wegard that as a widiculous question, Tom Mewwy. Nothin' is bitin' me,' answered Arthur Augustus. 'I am wathah surpwised at Talbot's extwemely bad mannahs — that is all.'

'Oh, bosh,' said Tom. 'Did you remind him that it's time to change?'

'Aftah his extwemely wude weception of me, I wefused to speak anothah word to him, Tom Mewwy.'

'Fathead!' said Tom.

'Wats!' retorted Arthur Augustus.

'What the dickens is the matter with Talbot?' exclaimed Tom. 'It's not like him to forget a football match. And that ass goes to look for him, and comes back without him.'

'I wepeat, Tom Mewwy —'

'Br-r-r-r!' grunted Tom. And he left the changing-room to go and look for Talbot himself, puzzled and not a little irritated.

He ran up the stairs to the Shell passage, and hurled open the door of Talbot's study. There was an angry exclamation within.

'Is that you again, you ass? Oh, Tom!' Talbot coloured, as he saw that the new-comer was Tom Merry, 'Oh, I thought it was that bothering ass D'Arcy again.'

'D'Arcy came up to tell you that it was time to change, if you're playing Soccer this afternoon,' said Tom, a little gruffly.

Talbot started.

'Oh! Did he? I'd forgotten —'

'You'd forgotten that we're playing Figgins and Co. this afternoon!' exclaimed Tom Merry. 'What on earth's the matter with you, Talbot?'

'Oh! Nothing.'

Tom gave him a quick, searching look. Then he came into the study and shut the door.

'What's the trouble?' he asked.

'Nothing! Only — I-I'd rather stand out this afternoon, if you don't mind, Tom.'

'I do mind!' said Tom.

'You can easily pick up another man —'

'Quite! While you mooch here in your study and brood?' asked Tom. 'Not good enough, old man. You're playing.'

'But — I-I —'

'Come off it!' said Tom. 'What's up?'

'You'd better get down to the football and leave me alone.'

'I asked you what's up? Nothing to do with that bad hat you saw a week or two ago — ? That blighter Purkiss — ?'

'No! No! He's gone, long ago, and I'd forgotten him.'

'Then what is it?'

Talbot stood silent. The look on his face told that he was plunged into the deepest despondency, and Tom was perplexed and concerned. He knew that the shadow of the past was never wholly lifted from the 'Toff': but generally Talbot was cheerful, kind, good-tempered: too fit and healthy, as a rule, to give way to despondency. But clearly he was in a black mood now.

'Give it a name, old fellow,' said Tom, his voice softening.

Talbot made a restless movement.

'I've been thinking, Tom — I-I think perhaps

it was a mistake for me to come here at all, and
that — that perhaps I'd better go.'

'Go!' repeated Tom, blankly.

'I'm out of place here,' muttered Talbot, moodily.
'There's always the past — and always a reminder
of it. Railton —'

'Railton?'

'It's that rotten affair of the prowler,' said Talbot, wearily. 'You remember Tom — I kept watch
a few nights ago — we talked it over, and I stayed
up — and Railton caught me, and — and supposed
that he had caught the prowler —'

'I know!' said Tom. 'But when you explained,
it was all right. Railton was satisfied about that.'

'Yes, yes! But —'

'But what?'

'Hasn't it struck you, Tom, that it's curious that
the prowler hasn't been heard of since that night?
He hasn't prowled since. And — and what is Railton to think?'

'Oh!' said Tom, slowly.

'What does it look like?' muttered Talbot. 'He
caught me out of my dorm — and the prowling
stopped from then. Tom, Railton can't help thinking, or at least suspecting, that he caught the right
man.'

'Oh!' said Tom, again.

'I've noticed him look at me, more than once, since!' muttered Talbot. 'I-I don't know what's in his mind, but — but what can he think, Tom? Nobody knows who that prowler was — nobody can guess what his game was. But if it was the Toff —'

'Talbot!'

'If it was the Toff, that explains it all!' said Talbot, with deep bitterness. 'If it was the Toff breaking out, it would be easy to think of a reason for him to be prowling at night — at the old game, Tom!'

Tom Merry shivered.

'That's what's on my mind — and I suspect on Railton's mind!' said Talbot, in a low voice. 'The prowling stopped — after he caught me! What does it look like?'

Tom shook his head.

'That's not in Railton's mind,' he said, decidedly. 'Whoever that prowler is, he knows now that the house-beak is looking for him — that's a good reason why he's stopped prowling. That's what Railton would think.'

'Perhaps!' said Talbot, slowly. 'But — but Tom, who was that prowler and what was his game?'

'I haven't the foggiest.'

'The way he rooted through the studies shows

that he was looking for something. What was he looking for?'

'Goodness knows.'

Talbot smiled faintly.

'You haven't lived my life, Tom,' he said. 'Suspicion doesn't come easily to you. Somebody prowls at night, spying in the studies and the dormitories — it's stopped, but it may begin again, and if anything was missing, Tom — and what else could be the prowler's object — ?'

'Oh!' gasped Tom.

'What could they think then?' muttered Talbot, his face dark and harassed. 'What could they think, except that the Toff was tired of a reformed life and had broken out again — in the old way?'

'Good heavens!' muttered Tom, aghast.

He stood looking at Talbot in silence. He realised now the weight that was on the Shell fellow's mind. But he shook his head.

'Wash it out, old chap,' he said, at last. 'You're letting it get you down — thinking too much about it. That prowler, whoever he is and whatever his game was, has chucked — and even if anything did happen, Railton couldn't and wouldn't think of you in connection with it. Look at it sensibly, old chap! If the Toff did break out again, the head-master's safe, or the money-drawer in Railton's

study, would be his game: not some trifle pinched
in junior studies or dormitories. Railton knows all
your history — he knows there isn't a lock in the
House that you couldn't open with your eyes shut—
if you chose to play the old game. If a pound note
or a watch was missing, it would be as good as
proof that the Toff had nothing to do with it.'

Talbot started.

Evidently that consideration, obvious as it was,
had not occurred to his troubled mind. There was
a long pause before he spoke again.

'Tom, old man, you've got more common sense
in your little finger than I've got in my head!' he
said, slowly. 'Could anyone suspect even the Toff
of petty pilfering — when he could help himself
from Railton's money-drawer if he liked?' He
shook himself, as if shaking away black doubts.
'Tom, I've been tormenting myself for nothing —
nothing —'

'Wash it out!' said Tom.

The study door burst open with a crash. Jack
Blake of the Fourth stared in.

'You men forgotten all about the football?' he
demanded. 'Are we playing the New House this
afternoon, or aren't we?'

Talbot laughed. He could laugh now.

'Just coming!' he said.

'Time you did!' grunted Blake.

'Come on!' said Tom Merry.

They followed Blake down the passage. The dark cloud had cleared from Talbot's handsome face. Once more, Tom Merry had proved a friend in need. Talbot looked his usual cheerful self as he came into the changing-room with Tom: and when they went into the field, he played up with all his accustomed zest. The cloud had rolled by: and neither Talbot nor his best friend could guess how soon it was to settle down again, dark and deep.

CHAPTER XVIII

BY WHOSE HAND?

'OH!' breathed Mr. Railton.

He started, as if he had been struck a blow.

He was in his study. Outside, the wintry sun gleamed in the quadrangle. Faintly, from a distance, came shouts from the football ground. A junior Soccer match was going on there.

A minute ago, Railton's face had been calm and kindly, as it usually was. He was seated at his study table, marking Latin proses, when the house-porter tapped at his door and entered. It was one of the innumerable little matters to which a house-master had to attend: the porter was going down to Rylcombe, where a small account had to be paid. Railton unlocked the money-drawer in his desk with the little steel key that had once been lost and found by Monty Lowther. Railton had been very careful with that key since: it had not been lost again — though certainly he had no suspicion of how narrowly he had escaped the japing propensities of the funny man of the Shell. Having unlocked and pulled open the drawer, he dipped into it for a batch of currency notes, in an elastic band, that lay there — or should have lain there. And then he ejaculated 'Oh!'

He stared into the open drawer.

The house-porter looked at him, across the table, wondering what was the matter. Railton's face was strangely startled. The man waited.

The house-master for the moment did not heed him. His eyes were fixed in an almost unbelieving stare on the money-drawer. The batch of currency notes was there — it had to be there! Only — it was not there!

It was gone!

'Oh!' repeated Mr. Railton.

Then he glanced at the house-porter.

'I will attend to the matter later,' he said.

'Very good, sir.'

The man left the study.

The door closed after him.

'Good heavens!' breathed Victor Railton, when he was gone. 'What-what-what does this mean? What can it mean?'

He drew the drawer out to its full length. There were many papers in it — letters, accounts, all sorts of papers. The house-master looked through them. He knew exactly where that batch of pound and ten-shilling notes should have been: but he examined the contents of the whole drawer to make sure.

The currency notes were not there. And his search revealed that something else was missing: a roll of bank-notes, ten in number, each for £5. Fifty pounds in bank-notes, thirty pounds in pound and ten-shilling notes, had disappeared, leaving no trace behind.

'Good heavens!' he repeated.

The sum of eighty pounds was missing from a locked drawer.

Railton's face was quite pale now.

There had been a robbery in his study. It must have taken place over-night. He had not had occasion to open the drawer that day, until now. But he had opened it the day before, and the money had been there, intact. It had been intact on Tuesday: it was gone on Wednesday.

Quietly, with set lips, he examined the lock of the drawer. There was no sign that it had been tampered with. The lock was intact — the drawer was intact. It had been opened with a key — or else by some skilled hand that did not need a key! His own key, he knew, had never left his possession since the day, a couple of weeks ago, when Tom Merry had returned it to him, after Lowther had found it on the stairs. It was the only key to that drawer. And it was not a common key or a common lock. It was a patent lock which no other key would fit.

'Good heavens!' said the house-master for the third time.

He knew what had happened — what must have happened. No key existed, excepting the one in his hand, that would unlock that drawer. The lock had been picked by some hand skilled in such nefarious work: the hand of a skilful cracksman. In all the crowd of fellows at St. Jim's there was only one capable of such nefarious skill, and to him it would have been child's play. That one was Talbot of the Shell: once known as the 'Toff' in the Angel Alley gang!

'No! No! No!' breathed the house-master.

He would not believe it.

He had had a surprise, a shock, the night he had found Talbot out of his dormitory in the dark while looking for the unknown 'prowler'. But the boy's explanation had satisfied him: it had been plausible enough. He had been struck, as Talbot surmised, by the fact that there had been no more 'prowling' since that night. But he would not let that weigh with him. He had trusted the boy and believed in him, as Dr. Holmes, the head-master, trusted and believed in him: as indeed all who came in contact with Talbot trusted and believed him. But now —

Only a practised cracksman could have unlocked that drawer without a key. Only the Toff —

'No! No!' repeated Mr. Railton. 'Never! Impossible!'

He closed the drawer again and paced his study, in a very agitated frame of mind. He would not believe that Talbot had done this. But if he had not, the thief must have come from without: there was no one but Talbot within the walls of St. Jim's who could have done it.

Was that it?

That surely was it. There had been no alarm in the night: no sign in the morning that the House had been entered. But a cracksman who could pick such a lock could deal with a window or a door without leaving a trace. Some skulking thief of the night had been there — that was it.

And yet —!

Victor Railton felt his heart sink, as he reflected. That money-drawer was known in the School House — plenty of fellows knew about it. But how could a thief from outside know anything about it? How and why had he selected that particular drawer in that particular study? What knowledge could any outsider have had of the interior arrangements in the School House?

Railton stretched out his hand to the telephone.
His impulse was to call up the police station at
Wayland, and ask Inspector Skeat to step over.

But he paused.

'If it was Talbot —!'

If that unhappy boy, not free after all from the
influence of his early surroundings and associates,
had done this —!

'No! No!' repeated Mr. Railton.

But he did not lift the receiver from the hooks.

He stood for long minutes in painful thought.
Then he crossed to the window and looked out.
Before he took any step — any step that could not
be retracted — he had to see the boy.

There were a good many fellows in the quadrangle, but Talbot was not among them. Kildare and
Darrel, of the Sixth Form, were chatting at a little
distance, and Railton called:

'Kildare!'

The captain of St. Jim's looked round.

'Yes, sir.'

'Please find Talbot and send him here, Kildare.'

'I think he's playing football, sir,' said Kildare.
'But if you want him at once —'

'No! Do not interrupt the game, if he is playing.
But send him here immediately it is over, Kildare.'

'Certainly, sir.'

Railton closed his window. He returned to his pile of Latin proses: but he found it difficult to concentrate on them.

CHAPTER XIX

INNOCENT OR GUILTY?

'GOAL!'

'Good old Talbot!'

'Bwavo, deah boy.'

'Goal! Goal!'

There was a crowd of juniors of both Houses round the football field. It had been a great game. Figgins and Co. of the New House had scored twice in the first half: and it was not till late in the second half that Tom Merry put the ball in for the School House. Then, as the game went on to the finish, it looked like a New House win: in fact, a whole crowd of New House men were all ready to utter a yell of victory. Lefevre of the Fifth, referee, was about to put the whistle to his lips. Perhaps Fatty Wynn, in the New House goal, had eased down a little, thinking the game as good as over. If so, Fatty had reason to repent it: for the ball came in from Talbot's foot, straight as a die, and Fatty clutched at it a second too late.

'Goal! Goal! Goal!' roared the School House crowd.

'Good old Talbot!'

'Toppin' deah boy! Weally, toppin'!' gasped Arthur Augustus D'Arcy: quite forgetful of his reception in Talbot's study earlier that afternoon. Talbot's manners might have deteriorated: but evidently his Soccer had not.

The whistle went.

'Good man!' said Tom Merry, clapping Talbot on the shoulder as they came off, 'Glad you played after all?'

Talbot laughed. His face was very bright — utterly unlike that of the moody fellow Tom had found in his study.

'Jolly glad!' he answered. 'Nothing like Soccer to blow the cobwebs away, Tom. And it's a draw with the New House, at any rate.'

'Fwightfully neah a win for them,' said Arthur Augustus. 'That chap Wynn is weally a wondah in goal — he stopped me evewy time —'

'Ha, ha, ha!'

'Weally you fellows —'

'Talbot!' It was the voice of Kildare of the Sixth, captain of St. Jim's.

Talbot looked round.

'Here, Kildare.'

'Go to Mr. Railton's study as soon as you have changed, Talbot,' said Kildare.

'Oh!' breathed Talbot. The brightness faded out of his face. 'Yes, Kildare — I won't be many minutes.'

In the changing-room, Tom Merry gave Talbot a rather anxious look. He could see that the summons to the house-master's study had startled and disturbed him.

'It's all right, old chap,' he whispered. 'Nothing to worry about, if Railton wants to see you.'

'I don't see why —!' muttered Talbot.

'Might be a dozen reasons. Don't take fences till you come to them, old fellow.'

Talbot nodded, without replying. He changed very quickly and left a cheery crowd behind him, when he hurried out. But his own look was not cheery. Railton had sent for him — why? There might be, as Tom had said, a dozen reasons: but his heart was heavy as he went to his house-master's study.

He tapped and entered.

Mr. Railton was sitting at his table, a pile of papers before him. But he was not giving them attention. His brow was wrinkled in deep and troubled thought. His eyes fixed on the junior as he entered, with a keen and searching glance. Talbot, as he met it, knew that his misgiving was well-founded — something was amiss. But he spoke quietly:

'Kildare sent me here, sir.'

'Yes Talbot! I have to speak to you.'

'Very well, sir.'

Railton was not in a hurry to speak. Talbot stood waiting, calm and quiet, but with a painful beating of his heart. It was, indeed, with a visible effort that the house-master spoke, at last:

'Talbot, something has happened here.'

Talbot waited for more.

'Something very serious — very serious indeed, Talbot. That is why I have sent for you. I must question you.'

Talbot drew a very hard breath.

'Will you tell me what has happened, sir?' he asked, very quietly.

'I must, Talbot. There has been a theft in this study.

Talbot started back.

'A theft, sir!'

'The sum of eighty pounds has been taken,' said Mr. Railton.

Talbot, after his sudden start, stood very still. Every vestige of colour had drained from his face. But he did not flinch under Mr. Railton's

searching eyes. The house-master's words had come
as a stunning blow to him. But he braced himself.
His face was white, but his eyes were steady. Slowly,
black bitterness came into his face. The house-
master sat silent, looking at him: and he spoke
at last.

'A theft in your study, sir?'

'Yes, Talbot.'

'And you send for me?' his eyes flashed. 'You
send for no other — but for me! I understand, sir!
I believed that you trusted me — I believed that
what I once was, was forgotten and forgiven —
I believed that you looked on me as a St. Jim's
junior like any other — but I understand now.
A theft has been committed and you think of me at
once — you remember at once that Talbot of the
Shell was once the 'Toff' — the associate of law-
breakers, the tool and dupe of lawless rogues. And
why should you not?' There was intense bitterness
in his voice and look. 'Why should you not? Why
should you believe that a boy, who fell among
thieves when he was a little kid, and knew no other
associations, could ever change — ever reform —
ever run straight?'

'Talbot!' exclaimed Mr. Railton.

Talbot's lip curled.

'There is your telephone!' he said. 'Call up Inspector Skeat — he knows my story, and will not be surprised to hear that the Toff has broken out again. Let him take me into custody and let me be charged with what you think I have done. I ask nothing at your hands, sir! I am ready to go — I should never have come here, and I am ready to go —'

'Will you let me speak?' exclaimed Mr. Railton. 'Listen to me, Talbot —'

The boy broke in, passionately.

'I will listen to nothing, sir! If you believe me to be a thief, call in the police, and charge me — that is your duty.'

'I must question you —'

'I will answer no questions. They are an insult.'

Mr. Railton breathed hard.

'Listen to me, Talbot. You do not know yet what has happened —'

'You have told me! Someone has taken eighty pounds from your study! You send for me — for me! For no other —!'

'Not because the money was taken, Talbot. Calm yourself! I should not have thought of you in connection with it — I trusted you too implicitly for that. It was the way the money was taken.'

'I don't understand —'

'The money was taken from this drawer, Talbot —

a locked drawer. I unlocked it to take something out — and found that the money was gone. The drawer was locked. The only key was in my keeping. The lock is an uncommon one — a patent lock. It was opened without a trace left. Who in this House, or in this school, could have manipulated a lock in that manner?'

Talbot almost staggered.

He realised then that it was not because of the shadowed past, not because of a lingering distrust of the 'Toff' that Railton had sent for him. It was because what had been done, could only have been done by one person in the school — the one-time 'Toff' of Angel Alley.

It was an overwhelming blow.

He stood looking at his house-master almost wildly.

'I did not distrust you, Talbot,' Railton's voice went on, quietly. 'My faith in you was firm. Had anything been taken from an open drawer, you are almost the last person in the House of whom I should have thought. But — a patent lock has been picked by a skilled hand. If this was done by any person inside the school, there is only one person capable of such skill, and you are that person. You must realise this.'

'I do!' said Talbot. 'I do! A lock has been

picked — a lock that nobody else at St. Jim's could pick — the fact speaks for itself! Who could have done that but the Toff?'

He gave a harsh laugh.

'I have sent for you, Talbot, to question you,' said the house-master. 'I have trusted you — I have believed in you — I have always been your friend, as you must know. And if old associations, old influences, have been too strong for you — if you have fallen to temptation, I can make allowances, every allowance, Talbot. But you must tell me. If some impulse, the result of your early training, has led you astray, tell me, and you will not find me hard.'

Talbot looked at him.

'You are very kind, sir!' he said.

'Have you anything to tell me?

'Yes, sir! I have this to tell you! I can tell you that, when I think of the past, it seems to me like an evil dream. I can tell you that when I was able to escape from it, when I was able to make good here, owing to your kindness, and the head-master's, and the friendship of Tom Merry, I was like a prisoner escaping from a dungeon. Looking back, I can hardly believe that I ever was the associate of such rogues as Hookey Walker and Smug Purkiss and the rest. You think I may have had an impulse,

a temptation, to go back to the old ways — you do
not understand, sir. I would die sooner! I would
die a thousand deaths sooner.' His voice rose passionately.

The house-master listened in silence, his eyes on
the boy's face.

'That is all I can tell you, sir!' said Talbot. 'If
you cannot believe me, the sooner I am gone from
this school the better.'

'I do believe you, Talbot!' said the house-master,
quietly. 'I had to question you — once the police
are on the scene the matter will be out of my hands.
You understand, of course, that this must go to the
police?'

'I understand that, of course, sir.'

'And you fear nothing?'

'Nothing.'

'I do — I must — believe you!' said Mr. Railton,
slowly. 'I cannot believe that I have been so de-
ceived in any boy — I have trusted you, and
I believe that I can trust you still. What has happened is almost inexplicable, if you are innocent:
but I shall believe in your innocence, Talbot.
Investigation will clear the matter up, I have no
doubt.'

He paused.

'For the last time, Talbot, think before you

answer — investigation must be thorough, and it will lead to the truth. You are sure that you have nothing to fear from it?'

'I have said so, sir.'

'Very well!' said Mr. Railton. 'You may leave my study, Talbot. I shall now call up Inspector Skeat.'

In silence, Talbot left the study.

When the door closed on him, Mr. Railton stretched out his hand to the telephone. But, as before, he withdrew it. His face was dark with painful thought. The boy was innocent — in spite of what looked like overwhelming evidence, he believed the boy innocent — he was determined to believe him innocent. And yet — and yet —

For a long time the house-master sat in thought: and at length he reached to the telephone again. And this time, he picked up the receiver and dialled Inspector Skeat's number at Wayland.

CHAPTER XX

THROUGH!

'COME on, old boy!'
  'No! I —'
  'Tea in our study.'
  'But —'
  'Barge him in!'
  'Ha, ha, ha!'
The Terrible Three were in great spirits. They
had reason to be. Two of them — Tom Merry and
Monty Lowther — had enjoyed a good game of
Soccer: and if that game had not been won by the
House, at all events it had not been lost. Manners
had not been in the School House team: but he
had enjoyed himself also, with his beloved camera.
The light that wintry day had been good, not only
for Soccer but for photography: and Manners had
a snap of Talbot in the act of kicking the equalising
goal, and several other snaps that afforded him
great satisfaction. So the three were merry and
bright and did not, for the moment, notice that
Talbot was not.

There was going to be tea in No. 10 in the Shell: and Talbot was going to join them: and they laughingly barged him along the passage to the study. They barged him in, and Lowther banged the door shut.

'Here we are,' said Monty. 'Aren't you ready for tea, Talbot, after urging the flying ball, as some jolly old poet puts it.'

'Oh! Yes! But —'

'Turning up your nose at our humble hospitality?' demanded Lowther.

'No! No! But —'

'We've got a cake — and sardines — and ham — and two kinds of jam!' said Lowther temptingly. 'Quite a feast of the gods! Trot out the viands, you fellows — and let the jolly old table groan under them!'

But Tom's eyes were on Talbot's face now. There was no smile on that face. It was pale — almost haggard.

'Shut up, Monty old man,' said Tom. 'Something's up! What's the row, Talbot?'

Monty Lowther became serious at once.

'Spot of trouble?' he asked.

'Yes — no — yes!' stammered Talbot.

'Kildare sent you to Railton,' said Manners. 'Not in a row with Railton, surely? Is that it?'

Talbot did not answer.

All the three were grave now. They could all see that something was amiss — very much amiss — with Talbot of the Shell.

'It's Railton?' asked Tom.

'Yes,' said Talbot, in a low voice.

'Not dragging up that prowler business again?'

'No! No! I-I suppose that was in his mind, too — but it's not that. I-I — Look here,' said Talbot desperately, 'I'd better cut — the less you fellows are mixed up with me now the better for you. I'm a dog with a bad name and you had better steer clear.'

He stepped to the door as he spoke.

Tom Merry caught him by the shoulder, and twirled him back.

'That won't do!' said Tom. 'We're all friends here, and if you're in a jam, we're the fellows to help.'

'Hear, hear!' said Lowther.

'Bank on that, Talbot,' said Manners, in his quiet way. 'We've been friends long enough, I think, for you to know that we'd stand by you, if you're in a jam.'

Talbot looked at them.

'I know you mean that,' he said, with a falter in his voice, 'and I'm grateful. But you can't help—

nobody can help — there's no help for me. Keep clear of me — that's your best guess. Before very long, nobody at St. Jim's will want to be known as a friend of mine.'

'Rot!' said Lowther, uneasily.

'Bosh!' said Manners.

'Forget it!' said Tom. 'You've done nothing to be ashamed of, or to make a friend ashamed — we all know that. Tell us what the row is.'

Talbot's pale face crimsoned.

'If I tell you, you'll wish you'd let me go,' he said. 'You won't — you can't believe in me, after I've told you.'

'For the love of Mike, what is it?' exclaimed Tom, in alarm. 'What's happened — we can see that something has.'

The crimson faded out of Talbot's face, leaving him white. But he did not speak.

'Tell us!' said Tom.

'You'll know soon anyway!' muttered Talbot, huskily. 'You'll know — all the House — all the school — will know, when — when —'

'When?' breathed Tom.

'When Inspector Skeat comes over from Wayland!' muttered Talbot.

'Inspector Skeat?'

'Yes!'

'In heaven's name, what's happened?' breathed Tom, his own face pale now. Manners and Lowther only stared blankly at Talbot.

'It's no use,' Talbot's voice was almost a groan. 'You couldn't believe me — you couldn't! Railton's trying to — but he can't quite! He's good and he's kind, and he's trusted me — but he can't help seeing how it looks! I can't help seeing it myself! If I told you, and you kicked me out of the study, I couldn't blame you. Better leave me alone.'

'What's happened?' repeated Tom.

'If you will have it — theft!' Talbot shivered as he spoke. 'Theft in Railton's study — eighty pounds missing —'

'Oh!' gasped the three together.

'Now you know!' muttered Talbot. 'And now — shrink away from me, as every other fellow will when he knows.'

'Don't be a fool!' Tom Merry's voice was rough. 'You can't mean that Railton suspects you — he couldn't! Is he mad, or what? Nobody's going to shrink away from you — every friend you have will stand by you, if Railton's mad enough to suspect —'

'Why should he not?' said Talbot. 'He knows what I was before I came here, as you fellows know —'

'I said don't be a fool!'

Talbot's pale face broke into a faint smile.

'You're a good pal, Tom!' he said. 'But even you couldn't face up to this — when you know.'

'You've told us —'

'I haven't told you all, yet. It's not only that the money's missing — Railton wouldn't suspect me only on that. It's the way it was taken,' Talbot pressed his hand to his forehead. 'That beats me, as it beats Railton — I could almost believe that I did it, the proof's so clear —'

'The proof?' exclaimed Tom.

'The money's missing from the money-drawer in Railton's desk. The lock was picked, without a sign on it that it had been touched. Who but the Toff could have done that?'

The three stood looking at him. Possibly, for a moment, there was a chill of doubt in their minds, as there was in Victor Railton's. They stood in silence, and Talbot's face contracted as he met their gaze — as if it gave him physical pain. His voice came haltingly.

'You made me tell you,' he muttered. 'You can't believe that I know nothing about it — you can't! Who else could have done it? Who else, in all this school had the skill, as well as the nerve? No one! Can you think of a single fellow capable

of it? You cannot — and I cannot! It was the
Toff's hand or nobody's that cracked that lock.
It's so clear that I could almost believe I had lost
my senses and gone back to the old ways, without
knowing it. I can't make it out! But — everyone
else will make it out easily enough — and Inspector Skeat will have no doubt. The Toff —
back to the old ways and the old days!' He laughed
discordantly.

'I believe you!' said Tom Merry, quietly. 'I can't
make it out, if it's as you say — but I can take
your word on it, Talbot.'

'Same here!' said Manners.

'And here,' said Monty Lowther. 'And I can
make a guess, too — that prowler who was lurking
about at nights last week —'

Talbot shook his head.

'Nobody knows who he was,' said Lowther, 'but
we know now what his game was — and that's it,
I tell you.'

Another shake of the head.

'If it had been a simple theft, yes,' said Talbot.
'But cracking a patent lock without leaving a
trace — I tell you, no St. Jim's man could do it, or
begin to know how to do it — only one — the one
who used to be called the Toff.'

'Oh!' said Lowther. And he was silent.

'But — what is Railton doing about it?' asked Tom.

'He's trying hard to believe in me. But he can't leave it where it is. He's calling in Inspector Skeat. He can't do anything else. It will not take Skeat long to make up his mind.'

'Perhaps!' said Tom, slowly. 'But — what you've said is true, Talbot — of all the fellows here, only you could have done it — and that means only one thing — that it was not done by a fellow here. It means that some miserable thief got into the House at night and robbed the money-drawer — that's what it means and what it can only mean.'

'It must — it must! But —'

'But what?'

'How's Railton to think so?' muttered Talbot. 'What would some thief from outside know about that particular drawer in that study? Whoever robbed that drawer had inside knowledge of this House, Tom.'

'Oh!' gasped Tom.

'Whoever the villain was, he knew exactly where to go. Who, outside this House, could know?' said Talbot.

Tom was silent.

'Outside the House, nobody could know—inside

the House, only one person could have done what was done!'

'Talbot!'

'That's the view Inspector Skeat will take — and what other could he take?' said Talbot, huskily. 'Tom, my game's up here. I'm through. Even you, old chap, will begin to doubt —'

'Never!' said Tom.

Talbot smiled faintly, and shook his head. There was no hope in his face — none in his heart. The 'Toff' had had a long and a hard struggle and it had ended — in defeat! He was through!

'I can't understand it at all,' said Tom, slowly. 'But you're not through, old man! Old Skeat is as keen as mustard — he will sort it out. It's a good thing Railton called him in — it's the duty of the police to find the guilty, and protect the innocent — and they do their duty, Talbot. You've got that to rely upon — and you've got to rely on it. Keep a stiff upper lip, old chap — we're going to see this through together.'

And those words of loyal friendship brought a glimmer of comfort, perhaps a glimmer of hope, to the tormented mind of the junior who felt himself entangled in a net from which there was no escape.

CHAPTER XXI

MR. SKEAT BLOWS IN

'BAI Jove!'

'What?'

'Bai Jove!' repeated Arthur Augustus D'Arcy. 'That is wathah wemarkable.'

'What is, fathead?'

'I wefuse to be addwessed as a fathead, Blake.'

'I wish you'd refuse to be one!' said Blake, 'but I suppose that's too much to expect.'

'Weally, Blake —'

'But what's biting you now, Gussy?' asked Herries.

'Nothin' is bitin' me, Hewwies, and I wegard the question as widiculous.'

The chums of Study No. 6 were sauntering in the quad, talking Soccer — playing the House match over again, as it were, when Arthur Augustus D'Arcy uttered that sudden ejaculation. In that match, Jack Blake had nearly, but not quite, landed the leather in the New House goal: and he was explaining to his friends how it really ought to have

183

been a goal though actually it hadn't been! Neither
Blake nor Herries nor Dig noticed what had caught
Arthur Augustus's noble eye and eyeglass, and
caused him to ejaculate.

'I wepeat,' said Arthur Augustus, 'that it is
wathah wemarkable. Whatevah is a policeman
doin' here?'

'A policeman!' exclaimed Blake, forgetting Soccer
for the moment, and even that goal that had so
nearly come off, but hadn't quite.

'At any wate, a police-inspectah!' said Arthur
Augustus. And he made a gesture in the direction
of Mr. Railton's study window.

Upon which his three chums all looked in that
direction. They then beheld the solid, stolid figure
of Inspector Skeat of Wayland: which was quite
well known to them by sight. And they stared at it.
Inspector Skeat of Wayland had been seen at the
school once or twice: but why he was there now was
quite a mystery to the chums of the Fourth. They
agreed with Arthur Augustus that it was rather
remarkable.

Mr. Skeat was standing outside the house-
master's window. He seemed to be making an ex-
amination of the window, the sill and its surroundings. The juniors watched him, with surprised
interest. Several other fellows were looking at him

from a distance, no doubt wondering, like Study
No. 6, why he was there.

The Wayland Inspector was taking no heed of
curious eyes. Perhaps he did not notice them. It
was more probable, however, that he did: for Mr.
Skeat was, as Tom Merry had said, as keen as
mustard. He was plump, he was ruddy: he was
solid and he was stolid: he had a rural aspect and,
at a careless glance, might have seemed not a
particularly bright member of the police force. But
there were some wrongdoers in the county of Sussex
who had found him too bright for them.

'What the dickens is he after?' said Blake,
puzzled.

'Must be after something,' said Herries, sapiently.

'Yaas, wathah.'

'Anything happened in Railton's study, I
wonder?' said Dig.

'Haven't heard of anything,' said Blake, 'But
that bobby's after something or other. He's going
over that window with a small comb.'

Cardew of the Fourth came along.

'You fellows know what's up?' he asked.

'Haven't the foggiest,' answered Blake. 'Old
Skeat seems to be jolly busy at Railton's window—'

'He's been busy at other windows,' said Cardew.
'He's been around some time. Lots of fellows have

spotted him at it. Can't have been a burglary?'

'Bai Jove!'

'Oh, my hat!' said Blake. 'Is that it? But we should have heard of it before now, if anything like that had happened last night.'

'Yaas, wathah.'

'It's a bit late in the day to send for a policeman, if anything happened last night,' said Digby.

'Well, something's up,' said Cardew. 'Railton must have sent for him, or he wouldn't be here. And he's not concentrating on that window just to pass the time. He's looking for clues, my beloved 'earers.'

'Couldn't be anything else, I suppose,' said Blake. 'Hallo,' he added, as four Shell fellows came along in a bunch. 'You chaps know anything?'

The four came to a halt.

Talbot was walking with the Terrible Three. He was in no mood for company, or indeed to show himself in public at all. His face was impassive — the 'Toff' was an old hand at concealing his thoughts and feelings. But it was grave: and his heart was heavy. But Tom Merry and Co. had walked him out after tea, with friendly insistence: and they chose to walk in sight of Mr. Railton's study window. They wanted the house-master to note that whatever might have happened, and whatever he might be thinking about it, it made no difference to Talbot's friends in his own form.

'Know anything?' repeated Monty Lowther, as Blake asked the question. 'Of course.'

Talbot's eye fell on the stolid figure at the house-master's window, and he had to repress a shiver. Tom Merry and Manners noted it, at the same moment, and they gave Monty a warning look. So far, nothing had been said of the occurrence in Railton's study: and unless the house-master made it public, Talbot's friends were only too anxious that nothing should be said. Monty Lowther caught the warning looks from his chums: but he acknowledged them only with a wink.

'Of course!' he repeated. 'What a question! Do we know anything? My dear chap, we know practically everything, in the Shell. When we were in the Fourth, we wallowed in ignorance like you Fourth-form kids, but in the Shell, we know all the answers —'

'You silly ass!' hooted Blake.

'Weally, Lowthah —'

'What do you want to know?' continued Lowther. 'Our stores of knowledge, acquired in a higher form, are at your service.'

'You funny ass, do you fellows know anything about that?' snorted Blake, and he indicated the inspector at the study window, with a nod of the head.

'That?' Monty Lowther glanced at Inspector Skeat. 'Certainly. That's a man —'

'What?'

'Genus homo, species sapiens,' said Monty Lowther gravely. 'Sub-species, police-inspector. Anything else you want to know?'

'Bai Jove! I wegard you as a sillay ass, Lowthah.'

'My dear chap, you are welcome to regard me in any character you care to assume,' said Monty.

'Weally, you funnay ass —'

'Lowther can't help being a funny fathead,' said Blake. 'Look here, you fellows, that bobby must be here for something. Bobbies don't go rooting round a building for nothing. Has anybody heard of anything missing?'

That was a question that the Shell fellows had no desire to answer. But Monty Lowther weighed in at once.

'Your silk topper safe, Gussy?' he asked.

'Weally, Lowthah —'

'And your trouser-press — ?'

'You uttah ass —'

'Missed any of your neckties?'

'Wats!'

'By gum, though, I've missed something this

afternoon!' added Monty Lowther, as if struck by
a sudden throught.

'You have?' exclaimed Cardew.

'Yes, rather — I've just remembered —'

'Anything valuable?' asked Blake.

'I should jolly well say so. It was something
I wanted more than anything else — and I missed
it this afternoon.'

The Fourth-formers were interested at once. Tom
Merry and Manners and Talbot stared at Lowther.
This was the first they had heard of Monty having
missed anything that afternoon.

'What have you missed?' asked Herries.

'Yaas, what was it, Lowthah?'

'Give it a name.'

'Tell us what you've missed.'

'Cough it up!'

It was an eager chorus of questions. Monty
Lowther smiled blandly as he answered:

'It was a goal!'

'What?' gasped Blake.

'A goal!'

'A goal!' repeated Arthur Augustus blankly.

'Just that!' said Lowther, with a cheery nod,
'It was in the House match this afternoon —
don't you remember, or didn't you notice, that
I got in a shot from the wing, and it hit a goal-post

and never found the net? I missed the goal —!'

'You silly ass!' roared Blake.

'Boot him!' snorted Herries. 'Lowther can't talk sense! Boot him.'

'Yaas, wathah!'

Monty Lowther dodged promptly.

'Come on, you fellows,' he said, 'these kids seem to have tired of our improving conversation. Trot!'

And the Shell fellows, smiling, trotted. Blake and Co. were left to speculate upon what might have called Inspector Skeat to St. Jim's.

CHAPTER XXII

THE INSPECTOR INQUIRES

'WELL?'

Mr. Railton asked that monosyllabic question.

Inspector Skeat sat in the house-master's study. His plump, stolid face expressed little. Railton's was troubled and anxious. Mr. Skeat did not seem in a hurry to speak. He was rather a ponderous gentleman, and slow — slow but sure.

'Well?' repeated the house-master.

'Nothing!' said Mr. Skeat.

'No trace?'

'No.'

'Does that mean that you regard this as what, in your profession, is called an "inside job", Skeat?' asked Mr. Railton, very quietly.

'That depends!' said Mr. Skeat. 'On the face of it, yes. So far as I have been able to discover there is no sign that this building was entered from outside last night. Your window, certainly, has not been tampered with; there is not a trace. On the other hand —' Mr. Skeat, always slow, paused.

'Yes, yes — what — ?'

'On the other hand,' said Mr. Skeat, 'the person who picked a patent lock so easily, without leaving a sign, was quite capable, if he chose, of dealing with a window, without leaving a sign that he had opened it and shut it again when he left.'

'That is very true,' said Mr. Railton, relieved, 'only —' he added, his brow clouding again.

'Only — ?' asked Mr. Skeat.

'Only why should he do so?' said Mr. Railton. 'Why should he take undue trouble when he could not have cared, after he was gone, whether we found a window open or not?'

'Obviously he must have had a reason if he took so much trouble to conceal the fact that the House had been entered,' said Mr. Skeat.

'What reason, then?'

'It might have suited his book to give an impression that it was an inside job. Who can tell?'

'Oh!' said Mr. Railton. Again he was relieved. 'Yes, yes, I see that. He would feel more secure — he would have less fear of pursuit by the police if he could make it appear that it was a theft by someone inside the House. That might very likely have been his reason.'

'That reason or another,' said Mr. Skeat. 'The fact that there is no trace of the House having been entered makes it look, at the first glance, like an inside job: but actually it proves nothing.'

Mr. Railton drew a deep breath.

'I am glad to hear you say that, Skeat!' he said. He paused a moment. 'Skeat, we have known one another a long time — we are, I hope, friends. You will feel for the position in which I am placed. I have told you everything frankly so that you may judge — but you will bear in mind that I have trusted that boy, and liked him, and trust and like him still. Your judgement in these matters is better than mine: but — but — but you will not allow yourself to be influenced by what you know of Talbot's past. You know his whole story — his whole miserable story —'

'I know!' said Mr. Skeat, 'and it will not influence me in the very least, sir. Circumstances are against the boy — some of his own making. When you found him out of his dormitory at a late hour he may have told you the truth —'

'I am sure that he did.'

'But you cannot know,' said Mr. Skeat, calmly. 'He may have told you the truth and he may not. If he told you the truth, that he was on the watch for some person who prowled the House at night, the whole affair is very singular. Is it a fact that any person did prowl at night?'

'That is certainly a fact,' said Mr. Railton. 'On
two nights last week, at least, some unknown person
prowled the House after lights-out. It was the talk
of the juniors at the time, and it was because some
of the talk reached my ears that I stayed up that
night, and —'

'And caught Talbot?'

'Yes.'

'Then we may take it as assured that there was
a prowler?' said Mr. Skeat, musingly.

'Undoubtedly.'

'He had never been found?'

'No.'

'You have no idea of his identity?'

'None.'

'Or a suspicion?'

Mr. Railton shook his head.

'None whatever,' he said. 'It is, as you have
said, a very singular affair altogether. Apparently, on at least two nights, some boy left his
dormitory and wandered about the House in the
dark. I have made some inquiries since, but they
throw no light on the matter. It appears that this
unknown person visited the Fourth Form dormitory
one night and the Shell dormitory the next: with
what object or intention is utterly unknown. He
appears also to have intruded into some of the

studies, both in the Fourth and the Shell —'

'Talbot's among the others?' asked Mr. Skeat.

'Yes, Talbot's among the others. Why?'

Mr. Skeat did not seem to hear the question. At all events he did not answer it. He wrinkled his brows in thought, and was silent.

The house-master waited for him to speak. He spoke at last.

'Did it occur to you, Mr. Railton, that this prowler, whoever he may have been, may have visited your study — this study?'

Railton started a little.

'No!' he answered, 'it did not occur to me. I can think of no reason why he should have done so.'

'You never found anything disturbed?'

'Not that I remember.'

'He seems to have left traces in other studies, or it would not be known that he had intruded there,' said Mr. Skeat, musingly. 'Did your inquiries go as far as such details?'

'From what I have gathered he seems to have meddled with the book-shelves chiefly — why, it is quite inexplicable to me.'

A sudden alert look came into the plump inspector's eyes.

'You are sure of that?' he exclaimed.

'So I have gathered,' answered Mr. Railton.

'The boys here write their names in their books, I have no doubt.'

'As a rule, yes.'

'Quite!' said Mr. Skeat. And he seemed to fall into a muse again.

A slight impatience became visible in Mr. Railton's manner. He had a great respect for Mr. Skeat and he knew that he was a capable officer of the law. But it did seem to him that the inspector was wandering strangely from the matter in hand. And as the inspector did not speak, Railton spoke.

'All this is leading us away from the subject,' he said. 'We are not inquiring into the foolish antics of a boy of this House, Mr. Skeat, but into the robbery that has taken place. Need we go into irrelevant matters?'

Inspector Skeat gave him a rather curious look.

'No detail is irrelevant, Mr. Railton,' he answered. 'From a hundred apparently irrelevant details a detective-officer will pick out the one that is relevant — and nothing is irrelevant until he has sorted them all out. However, let us return to our subject.'

'You have formed an opinion?' asked Mr. Railton, anxiously.

'I have an open mind, so far.'

'I am glad of that, at least!' said Mr. Railton,

relieved. 'I know how it looks — how it cannot fail to look. All the circumstances seem to condemn that unfortunate boy —'

'Not all of them,' said Mr. Skeat, stolidly. 'Some of them may have a bearing in his favour.'

'In what way?' asked the house-master, eagerly.

'We will go into that later, when I have more information for my guidance,' said Inspector Skeat. 'All is vague so far. I must see the boy, of course: but first you will give me exact details of the notes that are missing, currency notes and bank-notes. And then, perhaps, you will send the boy to me here, and leave me to question him.'

'As you wish!'

A few minutes later Mr. Railton left the study and Inspector Skeat was left alone, waiting for Talbot of the Shell to arrive, with a deeply thoughtful expression on his plump face.

CHAPTER XXIII

IN DOUBT

TALBOT came quietly into the study.

He had expected the summons, and he was prepared for it. His manner was quite calm and self-possessed. But his nerves were tense. He was like a fellow bracing himself to face a blow that could not be eluded: with little hope, but with courage.

The keen eyes in the plump, ruddy face searched him. Inspector Skeat had, as he had told the house-master, an open mind so far. Whether he was dealing with an unrepentant and cunning young crook, or with an unhappy boy who was the victim of circumstances, Mr. Skeat did not yet know. But he was going to know.

'You know why I am here, Master Talbot!' said the inspector, abruptly.

'I can guess, sir!' answered Talbot, 'and I can guess why you wished to see me. My house-master still trusts me as hard as he can in spite of what has happened here, but I cannot expect so much of an experienced police-officer.'

His tone was bitter.

'You will find a police-officer your best friend, if you are innocent in this matter,' said Mr. Skeat.

'There is no "if" about that.'

'You know nothing of what occurred in this study?'

'Nothing.' Talbot's lip curled. 'I know what it looks like. I wonder that Mr. Railton still clings to his faith in me.' He made a gesture towards the desk. 'Whose hand could have picked that lock but mine? Nobody's, at this school. Unless a thief penetrated the House in the night, from outside, who but I can be guilty?'

'There is no trace to be found of any such entrance.'

Talbot gave a hard laugh.

'I was not always Talbot of the Shell, Mr. Skeat, as you know only too well. I was once the Toff, of Hookey Walker's gang. I learned in a hard life to have my wits about me. If I had robbed that desk, traces would have been found of a forced entrance from outside — I should have taken care of that.'

Mr. Skeat nodded slowly.

'I had thought of that!' he said. 'I have thought of some other points, also, which may tell in your favour, Master Talbot.'

'Oh!' exclaimed Talbot, in surprise. 'Then I am

not condemned out of hand, Mr. Skeat? It is not a foregone conclusion in your mind?'

'By no means,' said Inspector Skeat. 'The law of this country is that every suspected person is innocent until he is proved guilty. Whether you are deceiving everyone at this school, and whether you have attempted to deceive me, is what I have to discover.'

'You?' said Talbot, inquiringly.

He felt the keen eyes searching and searching his face.

'Yes, me,' said Mr. Skeat, while Talbot stared at him in surprise. 'One day the week before last, Master Talbot, you have not forgotten that you telephoned to me. Whether what you told me was the truth or not I do not know.'

'Oh!' gasped Talbot.

'You gave me warning,' resumed the Inspector, 'that a lawless character you had known in other days was in this vicinity and that you had good reason to believe that he had designs on Wayland Grange.'

'I told you the truth.'

Talbot's pale face coloured. Mr. Skeat had, at the time, thanked him for the information given, and told him that measures would be taken. It had not occurred to him then that the Inspector had any doubts in his mind. But it seemed now that he had

not wholly placed faith in what he had been told.
The boy's lip curled bitterly. After all, why should
a police-inspector take the word of the Toff?

'The man you described, Smug Purkiss as he is
called, is well-known to the police,' continued Mr.
Skeat. 'He has served a term at Dartmoor for burglary: but since he came out of prison, there has
been no new charge against him. He is free to come
and go anywhere he may choose. But if you saw
him lurking about Wayland Grange after dark,
a very easy conclusion may be drawn.'

'If!' said Talbot. He breathed hard. 'I may tell
you, Mr. Skeat, that I consulted a friend here —
Tom Merry, the best pal a fellow ever had — before
I spoke to you on the telephone. I did not know
what to do, and it was on his advice that I telephoned you.'

Mr. Skeat nodded.

'No doubt, no doubt,' he said, 'but —'

'But you did not believe me?'

'I had an open mind,' answered Mr. Skeat,
calmly. 'We do not take things on trust, Master
Talbot. But I acted on the information you gave —
special watch was kept at Wayland Grange — if
Mr. Purkiss had made an attempt there he would
very soon have seen the inside of Dartmoor again.
But —'

'But no attempt was made,' said Talbot.

'Exactly.'

'Which cast doubt on what I had told you?'

'To some extent, yes.'

'And why,' said Talbot, 'why, if I had not known of Purkiss and his design on Sir Josiah Billing's safe, should I have telephoned to you at all, Mr. Skeat? Can you answer me that?'

'Very simply,' said Mr. Skeat. 'Your motive might have been to make a good impression on the police, to make it clear that whatever you once were you were now a friend of the law, anxious to prevent a crime — a very useful move in advance, Master Talbot, if you had it in mind to play the old game here.'

Talbot started violently.

'Oh!' he gasped.

'Quite a useful move, if that was the idea!' said Mr. Skeat, grimly. 'And it is a fact that no attempt has been made on Wayland Grange — but that a robbery has occurred at this school.'

'I — I have tried to do what was right.' Talbot's voice was husky. 'I had to prevent a crime. And it has placed the net round my own feet.'

'Let us have this clear,' said Mr. Skeat. 'You warned me of this man Purkiss and his design. If he had any such design why did he not carry it out?

Did he know that you had given warning of his intention?'

'That is easy, at least,' answered Talbot. 'He dared not, after the police had been warned to watch for him.'

'Did he know that?' repeated the Inspector.

'He did — for I told him.'

'Then you have seen him a second time?' Mr. Skeat's face was grimmer. 'You keep up this old acquaintance, Master Talbot, it seems.'

'Not by my choice,' said Talbot. 'The rogue had the nerve to telephone me here, on my form-master's telephone. He threatened to come to the school if I did not meet him outside. I could not face that.'

'And you met him?'

'Yes.'

'Where?'

'At the old hut in Wayland Wood.'

'I know the place — a very suitable spot for a very secret meeting!' said Mr. Skeat. 'And will you tell me what transpired?'

'I will!' said Talbot. 'I told him that his design was known to the police from information given by me, and that his best guess was to get out of the neighbourhood and stay out. In return he proposed that we should carry out the design at Wayland Grange together. My refusal enraged him, and he reiterated his threats to come to this school and do me all the harm he could. And then —'

'Then?' said Mr. Skeat.

'Then I warned him off by giving him the toughest thrashing he has ever had in his rascally life!' said Talbot. 'I left him lying on the floor of the hut, knocked out. That warning was enough for him. He went — and I have heard nothing from him since, and do not expect to hear anything.'

Mr. Skeat rubbed his chin thoughtfully.

'If that was what occurred, Master Talbot, you must have left him feeling very bitter — and revengeful!' he said.

'Very likely!' said Talbot, disdainfully. 'I do not fear him, or anything he might do.'

'If all this is correct —'

'If!' muttered Talbot.

'Yes, if!' said Mr. Skeat, stolidly, 'I am very much disposed, Master Talbot, to believe every word you say: but I have to consider other possibilities. You say you have heard nothing from Purkiss since?'

'Nothing.'

'And do not expect to hear anything?'

'No.'

'If you should hear from him —'

'It is not likely after what I gave him.'

'If you should hear from him,' repeated Mr. Skeat, as if Talbot had not spoken, 'can I rely on you to notify me at once?'

'Certainly,' said Talbot, 'if you wish, you shall know. I do not see the use, as you tell me that at present there is no charge against him. But if I get so much as a word from him you shall know at once.'

'Thank you,' said Mr. Skeat.

He fell silent.

Talbot waited: but the Inspector did not speak. He seemed to be buried in deep thought, almost as if he had forgotten that the boy was there. The minutes passed, and at last Talbot broke the silence.

'If you are through with me, Mr. Skeat —'

Mr. Skeat came out of his reverie.

'For the present, yes,' he said.

'Only for the present!' said Talbot, ironically.

'Quite!' said Mr. Skeat stolidly.

The junior made a movement to the door. Then Mr. Skeat spoke again.

'One moment, my boy.'

Talbot turned back.

'One more question,' said Mr. Skeat. 'Do you write your name in your school books, Master Talbot?'

Talbot stared at him in blank astonishment. It

was an utterly unexpected question: indeed, it almost seemed to him that the stolid police-inspector must be rambling. He was too astonished to answer for a moment or two.

'Well?' said Mr. Skeat.

'What can that matter?' exclaimed Talbot.

'I have asked you a question. Will you answer it?'

'Of course, but why — ?'

'Never mind why. Do you write your name in your school books?'

'Yes! Every fellow here does.'

Mr. Skeat nodded as if with satisfaction.

'That is all, Master Talbot! You may go.'

And Talbot, in wonder, went.

Inspector Skeat sat in deep thought after he had gone, his plump brow corrugated. A few minutes later the door opened and Mr. Railton came in. Then the Inspector rose to his feet.

'I have seen Talbot,' he said abruptly.

'And you have concluded — ?'

'No conclusion is possible yet,' said Mr. Skeat, slowly. 'On the face of it the boy is guilty. What has happened is merely what might have been expected — a boy brought up among dishonest associations has reverted to the old ways —'

'I cannot believe so.'

'There is no reason to believe so for the moment,'

said Mr. Skeat, stolidly. 'It is a matter of proof, one way or the other: and since you have called me in, Mr. Railton, it is my duty to furnish that proof, and I shall, I hope, do so. Either that boy is an honest and upright lad, the victim of circumstances — or else he is the most wary and cunning young rascal I have ever encountered in all my experience. At the moment I cannot say which.'

Mr. Railton compressed his lips.

'I think I can!' he said.

'Possibly! Possibly! But I incline to the former opinion,' said Mr. Skeat, tolerantly.

'I am glad of that at least.'

'But we shall see,' went on the Inspector. 'Only further developments can elucidate the facts of the case. The next move is up to you, sir.'

'To me?' said the house-master.

'Naturally! Money is missing, and Talbot is under suspicion. A search of his belongings is the next natural step.'

Mr. Railton made a gesture of repugnance.

'A distasteful task, no doubt,' said Mr. Skeat, 'but absolutely essential, sir. You have placed the matter in my hands, and I ask you to act on my counsel.'

'I shall do as you advise, of course — all the

more willingly because I am assured that such a search will reveal nothing to incriminate the boy,' said Mr. Railton, with emphasis.

The Inspector gave him a very curious look.

'You are assured of that?' he asked.

'Quite assured of it.'

'And yet —!' said Mr. Skeat, musingly.

'Yet what?' asked Mr. Railton, as he paused. But Mr. Skeat did not complete the remark he had commenced. Whatever was the thought in his mind he did not utter it.

'Well?' said Mr. Railton at last, with a touch of impatience.

'Well, we shall see — we shall see!' said Mr. Skeat. 'One more thing I must ask: it may surprise you but I must ask it. If the search should produce evidence against the boy —'

'I am sure that it will not.'

'If it should,' said Mr. Skeat calmly, 'I desire that it be kept secret for the present — that nothing whatever be said in public on the subject — even to the head-master, Mr. Railton — not a word to anyone.'

The house-master stared at him.

'I hardly understand you,' he said. 'No evidence could be found except the stolen notes —'

'Precisely.'

'In such an event the conclusion would be obvious.'

'Perhaps!'

'Did you say "perhaps"?' exclaimed Mr. Railton, blankly.

'I did.'

'Then I understand less than ever.' There was more than a hint of impatience in Railton's manner now. 'But seriously, Mr. Skeat, if, against my own belief and conviction, such evidence should be found, I must place the whole matter before Dr. Holmes at once —'

'I repeat, Mr. Railton, that I desire nothing to be said at the present stage,' he said. 'If you are not prepared to leave such matters to my judgement —'

'Of course, of course,' said Mr. Railton, hastily. 'But I must say plainly that I do not understand your object in the very least.'

'We have our own methods, Mr. Railton. I will say this much — that what I advise is in the boy's own best interests.'

'That is more than sufficient, Mr. Skeat — I will do exactly as you say.'

'Thank you, Mr. Railton! Whatever you may discover in Talbot's study or in his dormitory box or elsewhere, not a word until I apprise you that the word may be spoken.'

'Very well.'

'You will, of course, be very thorough in your search. I can rely upon you for that.'

'For the boy's own sake, Mr. Skeat, my search will be very thorough.'

'That is all then, Mr. Railton, for the present,' said the Inspector. 'I will take my leave. You will notify me of the result of the search by telephone.'

'Certainly.'

Inspector Skeat left the house-master of the School House a very puzzled man.

CHAPTER XXIV

MR. SKEAT WANTS TO KNOW

'MASTER Merry.'

'Yes, Mr. Skeat.'

The 'Terrible Three' were loitering in the quad, not in a happy mood, their eyes on the plump, portly figure that was coming away from the School House. Only too well they knew why Inspector Skeat was at St. Jim's: and why Talbot had been sent for to the house-master's study. They had not seen Talbot since, and were wondering rather dismally what had been the outcome of his interview with the police-inspector, when Mr. Skeat appeared, taking his slow and stolid way to the gates. Gladly the chums of the Shell would have asked him questions: but that, of course, they could not venture to do: and it was a surprise when Mr. Skeat stopped to speak of his own accord.

'I should like a few words with you, Master Merry,' said Mr. Skeat. 'Perhaps you will walk a short distance with me.'

'Certainly, sir,' answered Tom, in wonder.

Leaving Manners and Lowther staring, he walked out of gates with the plump Inspector. Mr. Skeat did not seem in a hurry to utter the 'few words' to which he had referred. He rolled on, plump and silent, and the schoolboy kept pace with him, wondering what was coming.

He spoke at last, his searching eyes turning on Tom's face.

'You are a close friend of the boy named Talbot,' he said abruptly.

'Yes,' said Tom, at once, 'His closest friend at St. Jim's, I think. No fellow ever had a better pal than Talbot, Mr. Skeat.'

The Inspector smiled faintly.

'You are acquainted with his history,' he said.

'Yes!' answered Tom. 'That makes no difference, Mr. Skeat.' Tom's eyes flashed. 'I know what has happened, Mr. Skeat, and that makes no difference either.'

'Talbot has told you —'

'He has.'

'I guessed as much,' said Mr. Skeat, calmly. 'That is why I desire to have a few words with you, Master Merry.'

'Go ahead,' said Tom. 'If you want to know anything about Talbot, Mr. Skeat, I can tell you

that he's one of the best in the school — straight
as a die, a splendid chap in every way.'

Mr. Skeat's smile broadened.

His keen eyes were on Tom. The schoolboy spoke
from loyal friendship to the suspected junior: and
that friendship, plainly, had not been shaken by
what he knew. He did not, and could not, believe
anything against his friend. It weighed with
Mr. Skeat: for Tom Merry was no fool: and he was in
daily, if not hourly, contact with the fellow who
had once been known as the 'Toff'. He knew Talbot
better than any other fellow knew him: yet evidently
he had seen nothing to shake his faith for a single
moment. This was one more point in Talbot's
favour, to be registered in Mr. Skeat's carefully-
calculating mind.

'Anything more?' asked Tom as the Inspector
rolled on in silence.

'Oh! Yes! Another matter,' said Mr. Skeat. 'It
appears that Talbot was caught out of his dormitory
one night by his house-master — a curious circumstance, Master Merry, in view of what has followed.'

'That's easily explained, Mr. Skeat,' said Tom
eagerly, 'some fellow had been prowling about the
House at night —'

'Who was it?'

'Nobody knows. Talbot kept watch for him and,

as it happened, Mr. Railton was up the same night and he caught Talbot out of the dorm — that's all.'

'Talbot was simply keeping watch for some unknown person who had prowled the House at night?'

'That is all, sir.'

'Did you know of his intention to keep watch?'

'Oh, yes, we talked of it in the study.'

Mr. Skeat gave Tom another very keen look.

'You are sure of this, Master Merry?'

'Of course,' said Tom.

Again Mr. Skeat walked on in silence. Tom waited for what was to come next. The Inspector spoke at last.

'It did not occur to you, Master Merry, that Talbot might have had some other motive for leaving the dormitory late at night, and that keeping watch for some prowler was a pretext.'

Tom set his lips.

'No!' he said, 'nothing of the kind. You don't know Talbot as I do, Mr. Skeat — you couldn't think that if you did.'

'I did not say that I thought so,' answered Mr. Skeat. 'I was merely stating a possibility.'

'Better call it an impossibility,' said Tom, curtly.

The Inspector smiled, and was silent again for a few minutes. But his slow voice same at last.

'You have spoken of some person prowling the

House at night, Master Merry. I have heard of this from Mr. Railton, as doubtless you may guess. It seems that his identity is unknown.'

'Quite unknown,' said Tom. 'Talbot might have caught him, perhaps, if Railton had not been up. But since then nothing's been heard of him.'

'The prowling has ceased?'

'It seems so,' answered Tom.

'The prowler remains unknown, and his motive unknown?'

'Yes,' said Tom. 'I can't make out who he was or what he was up to: but Talbot thought that he could be up to no good, and I agreed with him. We'd all have been glad to spot him and put a stopper on him.'

'No doubt!' assented Mr. Skeat. 'Can you tell me who first discovered that some person was prowling at night?'

'That was D'Arcy, in the Fourth,' answered Tom. 'He'd had a hack in a footer match, and it made him wake up, so I've heard. Somebody was in his dormitory, with a light, going from bed to bed —'

'As if in search of some particular person?'

'Well, it looked like it, from what D'Arcy has said, but I don't see why any fellow should —'

'All the boys have boxes in their dormitories?'

'Eh? Yes,' said Tom.

'Where is a boy's box placed?'

'At the foot of his bed.'

'Then if the person you call the prowler found a particular boy's bed he would be able to find that boy's box?'

Tom stared at the Inspector.

'Yes, I suppose so,' he said, 'but he wouldn't need to come at night for that — any fellow could dodge into a dormitory in the daytime and see anything he wanted to see —'

'Was the prowler seen again?'

'He was not seen,' answered Tom. 'Nobody's seen him. But he certainly prowled again, in my dormitory — the Shell.' Tom grinned at the recollection. 'Lowther got him with a squirt of ink, whoever he was. You see, we were expecting a Fourth-form chap to come larking, and Lowther sat up for him with the squirt — that was how it was! But it turned out afterwards that D'Arcy had gone to sleep and did not come till much later — so it must have been the prowler that got the ink.'

'Nothing has been heard of him since?'

'Nothing.'

'Did you not look for any boy with traces of ink on his person or his clothes?'

Tom Merry laughed.

'I think everybody did,' he answered, 'but he

must have cleaned it off very thoroughly in time —
nobody was ever spotted.'

'I understand that this prowler also made himself
busy in some of the studies at night,' said Mr. Skeat.

'He did,' answered Tom. 'An inkpot was knocked
over in Talbot's study —'

'Talbot's?'

'Yes, and other fellows found signs of him, too.'

'Books meddled with, for instance?'

'Yes — I can't imagine what his game was, but
he messed about with a lot of the fellow's books,'
said Tom.

'As the boys' names are written in their books
it would be possible to find any particular boy's
study by looking in the books,' suggested Mr. Skeat.

Tom Merry stared blankly at him.

'I suppose so,' he said, 'but that wasn't it —
couldn't have been — every fellow in the House
knows every fellow's study without looking in his
books to find out.'

'Of course, of course,' said Mr. Skeat. 'No
resident in the House would need to do anything
of the kind.'

'Hardly,' said Tom.

'Do you know whether any of Talbot's books
were messed about, as you call it?'

'Oh, yes,' said Tom. 'I remember his Virgil was

taken off his book-shelf and put back in a different place.' He laughed, 'But the prowler couldn't have been looking for his name in his book to find out if that was his study, Mr. Skeat — every man in the House knows Talbot's study.'

Mr. Skeat nodded.

'Every man in the House!' he repeated. 'Yes, yes, quite so. A very mysterious matter, this of the prowler, Master Merry.'

'It beats us,' said Tom, 'but you can bank on it, Mr. Skeat, that this prowler, whoever he was, was not Talbot. Talbot was in bed in my dorm when Lowther got the prowler with that squirt of ink.'

'You are sure of that?'

'Yes: he sat up and spoke.'

Mr. Skeat walked on in silence again. He seemed to have nothing more to ask the puzzled schoolboy. He stopped at the stile in Rylcombe Lane, beyond which lay his way by the footpath to Wayland.

'Thank you very much, Master Merry,' he said. 'Good-bye.'

'Good-bye, sir!'

Mr. Skeat lifted his solid weight over the stile and disappeared up the leafy footpath. His plump brow was corrugated with thought as he went. Tom Merry would have been surprised, and interested, could he have followed the Inspector's thoughts.

'A prowler at night — a foolish boy's antics, or — or some person from outside seeking his bearings — seeking knowledge of one boy's quarters — for what object?' So ran Mr. Skeat's thoughts. 'Some person with a grudge against the boy, intending harm — and if Talbot has told me the truth, there is — or was — such a person. But — but — only the boy's word so far, and the boy was once the "Toff" —!' Mr. Skeat shook his head slowly and ponderously. 'We shall see — we shall see! So far, an open mind!'

Mr. Skeat rolled ponderously on, thinking it over. So far Mr. Skeat had 'an open mind'. But Mr. Skeat was, as Tom had told Talbot, as keen as mustard: it was the duty of the police to find the guilty and to protect the innocent: and that duty Mr. Skeat was going to do. Slow and stolid as he looked, Mr. Skeat had his teeth into this: and whatever was the truth of the strange affair, Mr. Skeat was going to worry it out.

Tom Merry walked back to St. Jim's in a puzzled frame of mind. Manners and Lowther were equally puzzled when he told them of his talk with Mr. Skeat.

'He seemed more interested in our prowler than in anything else,' said Tom. 'Blessed if I know why. Some silly fathead playing tricks after lights-out —

and he's chucked it now, anyway. Seen Talbot about?'

'Just gone into the House with Railton,' said Manners.

'I wonder —!' said Tom.

They all wondered why Railton had called Talbot into the House. It would not have conduced to their comfort if they had known why, and what was to follow.

CHAPTER XXV

A STARTLING DISCOVERY

SKIMPOLE of the Shell blinked up in surprise
from the entrancing pages of 'The Gaseous Origin
of Mind and Matter'. The door of No. 9 study in
the Shell had opened and he expected to see either
Gore or Talbot, but it was his house-master,
Mr. Railton, who entered. A moment later, however, Talbot followed the house-master in.

Railton glanced at the brainy man of the Shell,
blinking over his ponderous volume.

'Kindly go down, Skimpole,' he said, briefly.

'Eh? Oh! Yes, sir!' bleated Skimpole, still more
surprised. Why Railton had come to the study at
all was a mystery to Skimpole: and why he told
Skimmy to go down was another mystery. However, Skimmy had to do as he was told: and he
picked up 'The Gaseous Origin of Mind and
Matter', put it under his arm, and left the study
to concentrate on the enthralling pages down in
the day-room.

'Close the door, Talbot,' said Mr. Railton.

Talbot, in silence, shut the door of the study after Skimpole. His face was set.

There was a momentary silence in No. 9. Talbot stood waiting. It was the house-master who broke the silence. He seemed to speak with reluctance.

'I am here to search your study, Talbot!' he said.

For a moment Talbot's eyes glinted, but it was only a moment. He reflected bitterly that the 'Toff' could expect nothing else. His manner was very quiet.

'I guessed that, sir, when you told me to come up!' he answered dryly.

'I desire you to be present during the search, Talbot. That is only fair to you.'

'Thank you, sir.'

'You have no objection to a search?'

Talbot's lip curled.

'If I had, would it make any difference?' he asked bitterly.

'I have asked you a question,' said Mr. Railton sharply.

'Very well, sir — I have no objection.'

'I was sure that you would have none,' said Mr. Railton more kindly. 'You must not suppose that this indicates suspicion or distrust on my part, Talbot. I am acting on official advice. The matter is now in Inspector Skeat's hands, and he requires a search to be made. That anything will be found to your discredit I am assured will not be the case.'

'Thank you, sir!' said Talbot again.

'It is a distasteful task, but I have no choice but to go through with it in the most thorough manner,' said Mr. Railton.

'I understand that, sir.'

'You share this study with two other boys,' went on the house-master. 'Gore and Skimpole could not, of course, be in any way concerned. You will point out your own belongings, Talbot, for me to examine. Have you any kind of receptacle here which your study-mates never use?'

'My desk, sir.'

'Please open it.'

Talbot opened the desk, unlocking it. Many things, in junior studies, were used in common: but obviously if purloined notes were hidden in the study they could not be left where Gore or Skimpole might have chanced on them. The locked desk was the only possible place.

There were papers, half-finished exercises and so on, in the desk. In several little pigeon-holes there were note-paper and envelopes. One of the pigeon-holes was quite full, stuffed with old letters.

Talbot stood watching the house-master as he proceeded to search through the contents of the

desk. There was a bitter smile on his handsome
face. He owed this humiliation to Inspector Skeat:
he knew that. In his interview with the Inspector
he had had an impression that Mr. Skeat had, as
he had said, an open mind on the subject. This did
not look like it!

Mr. Railton proceeded quietly but very thoroughly with the search. He left till the last the
pigeon-hole stuffed with old letters. But he came
to it at last, and drew out the crumpled letters one
by one.

Then Talbot saw him give a sudden start.

His hand was stretched into the pigeon-hole but
he drew it back as if a snake had stung it.

The colour changed in his face.

'Good heavens!' he exclaimed.

Talbot stared at him blankly. What was the
matter with Railton? He could have found nothing
but old letters in that pigeon-hole. Yet the house-
master stood looking like a man stunned.

Talbot made a step towards him.

'Mr. Railton — what — what is the matter?
What — ?'

The house-master turned his head and looked at
him. His look made Talbot's heart beat unpleas-
antly. There was surprise in it — surprise and
sorrow and scorn. What could it mean?

'Talbot!' Railton's voice seemed changed.

'Yes, sir! What —'

'You alone use this desk?'

'Certainly, sir.'

'You keep it locked?'

'Yes.'

'You do not leave the key about?'

'I keep it in my pocket, sir.'

'No one else, then, could have access to this desk?'

'No one, sir.'

'Whatever is in this desk, Talbot, was, and must have been, placed there by your own hand.'

'Certainly, sir,' said Talbot, in utter wonder.

Railton gave him a long, hard look. Then he stretched out his hand again, into the pigeon-hole in the desk. He drew out something from that pigeon-hole: something that had been hidden there behind the old letters stuffed in after it. Talbot looked, and staggered.

He did not believe his eyes for a moment. For what Mr. Railton drew out of that hiding place was a wad of currency notes — pound notes and ten-shilling notes, fastened together with an elastic band.

He stood unsteadily, staring.

With a grim, hard face the house-master examined the notes. There were twenty pound notes, and twenty of ten shillings: thirty pounds in all. It was hardly necessary for Railton to examine them. He knew that the notes were those that had been taken from the money-drawer in his study. No junior at St. Jim's was likely to have such a sum in his possession of his own.

'Talbot.' His voice was hard.

Talbot panted.

He could not speak. He could only pant for breath, staring wildly at his house-master. He could scarcely believe what he saw. The wad of notes in Railton's hand seemed to dance before his eyes.

'Talbot! This is not your own money. Dare you say that you have such a sum as thirty pounds here of your own?'

Talbot found his voice.

'No!' he gasped, 'I have never had such a sum. I don't keep money in that desk at all. What I have is in my wallet, in my pocket.'

'I have here thirty pounds in currency notes!' said Mr. Railton. 'I find them stuffed in a pigeon-hole, hidden by a heap of old letters stuffed in after them. The money is not your own.'

'No!' muttered Talbot, huskily.

'It was taken from my study by a thief in the night. I find it here — hidden in your desk.'

'I — I — I —'

He did not believe his eyes for a moment

'You need say nothing, Talbot. I believed —
I trusted in you — I believed that a search could
only prove that nothing could be found here that
did not belong to you. And this is what I have
found.'

'I — I — this must be some horrible dream!'
panted Talbot. 'I — I never knew the notes were
there, sir — I never knew — I did not put them
there — I have never seen them before — I — I —'
His voice trailed away under the house-master's
stare of scorn.

He knew, while he spoke, that Railton could not
believe him. The stolen notes were there, hidden
in his desk of which he alone had a key. No one but
the Toff could have picked the lock in Railton's
study: no one could have unlocked that desk: and
what became now of the theory that some nocturnal
thief outside the school had penetrated the House,
under cover of night? A midnight thief would not
leave his plunder behind him!

'That will do, Talbot,' said Mr. Railton, and his
tone was cutting. 'I have only one word more to
say. Where are the bank-notes?'

'The — the bank-notes?' stammered Talbot.

'Fifty pounds in bank-notes were taken from the
money-drawer in my study, as well as these
currency notes. They were taken by the same hand.

I do not find them here. What have you done with them?'

'I know nothing —'

'Where have you hidden the bank-notes?'

'I know nothing about them — I have never touched them — I — I —'

'Silence!' exclaimed Mr. Railton angrily, 'I shall search your box in the dormitory, Talbot, and have little doubt that I shall find the bank-notes there. If you refuse to tell me —'

'I have nothing to tell you. I —'

'Silence!'

With that, and a last look of scorn, the house-master crossed to the door and left the study. He left Talbot standing with a face white as chalk, his brain in a whirl, wondering dazedly whether this was some fearful dream from which he would awaken.

CHAPTER XXVI

GUSSY THINKS IT OUT

'I'VE been thinkin' —'

'Gammon!'

'Weally, Blake —'

'Don't pile it on, Gussy,' said Blake, shaking his head, 'We'd take your word on anything else, but that's too steep.'

Herries and Dig chuckled.

'You uttah ass!' said Arthur Augustus, in measured tones. 'I wepeat that I have been thinkin' —'

'And I repeat that it's too steep!' said Blake, with another shake of the head. 'What did you do it with, if you come to that?'

There was another chuckle from Herries and Dig. The expression on Arthur Augustus's aristocratic countenance seemed to amuse them.

Study No. 6 had been discussing Inspector Skeat's visit. It had excited a good deal of curiosity among the St. Jim's fellows who had seen him 'pottering' about the House. Blake and Co. could not help wondering why he had been there. Dozens

of fellows knew that he had pottered about the
House examining doors and windows: and that
afterwards he had been for some time in Mr. Railton's study. That was all they knew: with the single
exception of Talbot of the Shell. Arthur Augustus's
announcement that he had been 'thinkin'' did not
impress his comrades unduly. Their faith in the
efficacy of Gussy's thinking processes was absolutely nil.

'I wathah think that I am the bwainy man of our
study, Blake,' said Arthur Augustus, 'and I wathah
think that I have spotted what is the mattah. Old
Skeat did not come here for nothin' —'

'Hardly!' agreed Blake.

'Somethin' must have happened —'

'Something!' Blake agreed again.

'Somethin' in Wailton's study, as it was Wailton
sent for him,' said Arthur Augustus. 'So fah as
I know he has not seen the Head! It is somethin' to
do with Wailton.'

'You've really thought that out?' asked Blake.

'Yaas, wathah.'

'Marvellous!' said Blake, 'it's clear as daylight —
perhaps that's why you were able to think it out,
old chap.'

Once more Herries and Dig chuckled.

'Pewwaps you will allow me to continue without

fwivolous intewwuptions,' said Arthur Augustus with dignity. 'Somethin' has happened in Wailton's study to make him call in a police-officah. It must be somethin' that he wegards as vewy sewious.'

'Sort of!' assented Blake.

'And I wathah think I have spotted what it is!' said Arthur Augustus. 'That ass Lowthah has been playin' twicks again. You know that once he put gum in my toppah, and on anothah occasion he sewed up my twousahs in the dorm —'

'Ha, ha, ha!'

'Weally, you fellows —'

'Oh, crumbs!' said Blake, 'you think Railton would call in a bobby if a funny ass put gum in his hat —'

'Nothin' of the kind, Blake. It is more sewious than that. One day last week those Shell chaps were wowin': Lowthah was vewy watty because they had stopped him playin' a twick in Wailton's study — he was vewy watty, and he was callin' them wet blankets for spoilin' a jape on the house-beak, and what do you think that jape was?'

'Give it up!' yawned Blake.

'It appeahs that Wailton had dwopped the key of his money-dwawah, and Lowthah found it: and you know what a japin' ass he is — he actually had the ideah of takin' Wailton's bank-notes out of the

dwawah and hidin' them in Wailton's study, to
give him a hunt for them —'

Blake whistled.

'Mad as a hatter!' he said. 'Lowther all over.
Lucky for him his pals put the stopper on — he
might have got into a fearful row.'

'Yaas, wathah! Tom Mewwy and Mannahs seem
to have stopped him, and he was not able to cawwy
on with it. But I heard him say that if he found
Wailton's key again he would cawwy on and not
tell them till aftahwards. That,' said Arthur Augustus, 'is what I have been thinkin' out. If Lowthah
played such a twick in Wailton's study, what could
Wailton think except that the bank-notes had been
taken — and send for a policeman?'

'Oh, crumbs!' said Herries.

'By gum!' said Digby, 'it looks like it — Railton
wouldn't call a bobby here unless something serious
had happened — and if he's missed bank-notes he
jolly well wouldn't guess that it was only a mad
jape.'

'Of course he wouldn't,' said Blake, 'but —'

He whistled again.

'I wathah think that it will turn out to be nothin'
but a pwactical joke of that funnay ass Lowthah,'
said Arthur Augustus. 'It would have happened
before if his fwiends hadn't stopped him, and now—'

'D'Arcy!' A sudden voice interrupted Arthur Augustus, and he looked round. The four juniors, in a group by the old elms, had not noticed a fellow leaning on a tree with his hands driven deep in his pockets, and a cloud of deep and harassed thought on his brow. Talbot of the Shell came quickly towards them as he spoke so suddenly.

'Yaas, deah boy,' said Arthur Augustus, turning his eyeglass on Talbot.

The chums of Study No. 6 looked very curiously at Talbot. He did not seem much like the cheery fellow who had kicked the equalising goal in the House match that afternoon. His face was sombre: his eyes almost haggard. Almost stunned by Railton's discovery in his study, Talbot had been trying to think it out — but thinking it out only left his brain in a whirl. What had happened was inexplicable — impossible — yet it had happened. The talk of the four juniors had passed him by unheeded — till now. Now he came eagerly towards them.

'I heard what you were saying, D'Arcy —!' he almost panted.

'You are vewy welcome, deah boy,' answered Arthur Augustus. 'Nothin' to get excited about, is there?'

'Oh! Yes! No! But you were saying that Lowther

had been playing silly tricks in Railton's study —
hiding his bank-notes —'

'Not pwecisely, Talbot! He was goin' to do so
only Tom Mewwy and Mannahs stopped him. I was
wemarkin' that it looks to me as if he has been
playin' that fatheaded pwactical joke on Wailton,
as the house-beak has called in a policeman.'

'Could any fellow be such a fool?' muttered
Talbot.

'Oh, Lowther all over,' said Blake. 'He never
stops to think before he goes for a jape. Lucky for
him his pals have more sense.'

'Yaas, wathah! A fellow who would put gum in
a fellow's toppah would stop at nothin' in my opinion,' said Arthur Augustus.

'You are sure that he had the idea — ?'

'Quite, deah boy — I heard them talkin' about
it, and Lowthah waggin' Tom Mewwy and Mannahs for stoppin' him. You see, I had gone to their
study to put some gum in the arm-chair, just to
show Lowthah that his own sillay twicks might
come home to woost, and they came in, and I dodged
behind the door knowin' that they would cut up
wusty. And they did,' added Arthur Augustus, 'they
actually had the fwightful nerve to sit me down in
the gum in the arm-chair —'

'Ha, ha, ha!' yelled Blake and Herries and Dig.

'Weally, you fellows, it is hardly a laughin' mattah,' exclaimed Arthur Augustus warmly, 'my twousahs were pwactically wuined —'

'Ha, ha, ha!'

'Oh, wats!' said Arthur Augustus. 'So you see, Talbot — bai Jove, where are you goin', deah boy?'

Talbot did not answer. He was hurrying away towards the House. Blake and Co. stared after him as he went.

'What the dickens is the matter with Talbot?' said Herries.

Arthur Augustus shook his head sadly.

'I feah that his mannahs are detewioratin',' he said. 'Several times lately he has been vewy bwusque, and now he wushes off while a fellow is speakin' to him without waitin' for a fellow to finish his wemarks. He used to have vewy good mannahs indeed: but I feah vewy much that they are detewioratin'. Howevah, as I was sayin' —'

And Arthur Augustus resumed his remarks, with Blake and Herries and Dig as more or less attentive listeners, while Talbot of the Shell disappeared into the School House.

CHAPTER XXVII

WAS IT LOWTHER?

'LOWTHER —'

'Adsum!'

'Was it you?'

'Eh?'

'You ass — you dummy — you fathead — was it you?'

Monty Lowther fairly blinked. Tom Merry and Manners stared. The Terrible Three were in their study when Talbot of the Shell burst in — hurling the door open wide and coming into the study rather like a whirlwind.

His face was flushed, his eyes sparkling. Never before had the chums of the Shell seen that usually quiet and reserved junior in a state of such excitement. They were utterly taken aback and amazed. They could only stare.

Talbot, in his excitement, caught Monty Lowther by the shoulder and almost shook him. What he had heard from D'Arcy had seemed, at least, to let in light on the incomprehensible happening in his own study. His eyes blazed at the astounded Monty.

'Will you answer me?' shouted Talbot. 'Was it you?'

'Gone mad?' gasped Monty Lowther.

'Answer me.'

'Talbot, old man —!' exclaimed Tom Merry.

'What on earth —!' exclaimed Manners.

'I want an answer, and I want it at once. Was it you, you japing, silly, irresponsible idiot?' shouted Talbot.

'Let go my shoulder.'

'Answer me!'

'I'll punch your cheeky head if you don't let go! What the dickens do you mean?' exclaimed Monty Lowther, 'bursting into a fellow's study like a wild Indian and grabbing him —'

Talbot made an effort at self-control. His hand dropped from Lowther's shoulder. He stood panting.

'For the love of Mike what's the matter, Talbot?' exclaimed Tom Merry. 'What has Monty done — or what do you think he has done?'

'Some jape in your study?' asked Manners, in wonder.

Talbot gave a savage laugh.

'I dare say that born idiot would call it a jape,' he snapped. 'A fellow mad enough to play tricks with money might think anything. If Lowther has done this for one of his mad practical jokes —'

'What have I done?' yelled Lowther.

'Can't you tell us what's happened?' exclaimed Tom Merry.

'Yes, I'll tell you. You know that money has been taken from the drawer in Railton's desk in his study — you know that Inspector Skeat has been here from Wayland — you did not know that he advised Railton to search my study —'

'Oh!' exclaimed Tom.

'Nothing to do with me, I suppose?' snapped Monty Lowther.

'That's what I want to know. I've just heard about a mad jape you planned on Railton — taking the bank-notes from his drawer and hiding them — did you do it?'

'Oh, that!' said Tom Merry. 'Lowther never did it — we stopped him. That was a couple of weeks ago —'

'I know that! But has he done it since? That's what I want to know, Monty Lowther. If you were fool enough to think of doing it then, you are fool enough to have done it last night. Did you?'

'Oh!' gasped Lowther.

'Don't be an ass, Talbot,' Tom Merry spoke almost roughly, 'Lowther did nothing of the kind—'

'How do you know he did not?'

'Because he couldn't have. He had picked up Railton's key: but I took it back to Railton at once, while Manners kept him here in this study. Railton has had his key ever since.'

'If he dropped it once he might have dropped it again. I want to know whether Lowther took out those bank-notes and hid them, as he intended to do.'

Manners gave a whistle.

'Monty, you ass,' he exclaimed, 'you never —'

'Of course I never did!' howled Lowther. 'Think Railton would put that key in a pocket with a hole in it after losing it once? I've never seen it since Tom took it back to him. Think I could open that drawer without the key?' added Lowther, with angry sarcasm. 'I haven't had the experience that some fellows here have had.'

'Shut up, Monty!' exclaimed Tom hastily. 'Look here, Talbot, cool down. Lowther's not even seen that key since I took it back to Railton. What on earth's put this idea into your head?'

'Some of the notes have been found —'

'Found?' exclaimed Tom.

'Yes, hidden!'

'In Railton's study?' asked Manners.

'No!' said Talbot huskily.

'Where then?'

'In mine.'

'Good heavens!' breathed Tom Merry.

There was a stunned silence in No. 10 study. Talbot stood breathing hard, the Terrible Three gazing at him blankly.

'Found — in your study!' said Tom at last. 'Is — is that what you said, Talbot?'

'That is what I said.'

'But — it's impossible!'

'Railton found a wad of currency in my desk — thirty pounds. The notes taken from his money-drawer last night.' Talbot's eyes gleamed at Monty Lowther. 'You were going to take out those notes and hide them, Lowther — that's your idea of a jape. Did you — ?'

'Lowther, you couldn't be such a mad ass — !' breathed Manners.

Monty Lowther crimsoned.

'You know what I was going to do,' he panted. 'I was going to hide them in Railton's study and give him a hunt for them. It was a potty idea — I can see that now. But that was all. Think I should be fool enough, idiot enough, rotter enough to hide them in another fellow's study?'

'You're fool enough, idiot enough, if not rotter enough to do anything for a mad practical joke,' said Talbot. 'You couldn't open Railton's money-drawer without the key — it's a patent lock — but if you had the key —'

'I hadn't!' yelled Lowther.

'Don't you keep your own desk locked, Talbot?' asked Manners quietly.

'Yes! But that's a common lock — any fellow with a bunch of keys could find one to fit it. Somebody got those notes and put them in my desk. Railton found them there. You know what that means to me! Railton has condemned me already. I shall be taken to the Head and sacked.' Talbot clenched his hands, 'And all the while it may be only a mad practical joke — no doubt it would seem funny to Lowther for the Toff to be suspected of breaking out again —'

'It wouldn't, Talbot,' said Lowther, very quietly. 'I tell you I've never seen Railton's key since Tom took it back to him — and I wouldn't play a trick like that on you, or any fellow, to save my life. If you can't believe me you must please yourself.'

'The notes were in my desk!' said Talbot. 'I did not put them there. I'd never seen them till Railton found them. Who put them there?'

There was no answer to that.

Talbot looked from face to face. His own face whitened.

'If it's not, after all, a mad trick of Lowther's —'
he muttered.

'It's not!' said Tom.

'If it isn't —'

'No "if" about that,' said Manners. 'It isn't.'

'Then — then you must think — you must believe — as Railton does — now I've told you. I've
told you the notes were found in my desk — hidden
in a pigeon-hole behind a lot of old crumpled
letters. Hidden there by the same hand that took
them from Railton's money drawer. If it was not
Lowther —'

'It was not!' said Lowther quietly.

Talbot set his lips.

'If it was not you it was I,' he said. 'It was not I!
I can't believe you, Lowther. You played this insane
trick and it's up to you to own up to it. I can't
believe you.'

With that Talbot strode out of No. 10 study.

He left the chums of the Shell looking at one
another in dead silence. Monty Lowther broke it.
His voice was unsteady.

'I was a fool — a fool —!' muttered Lowther.
More than once Monty had had reason to repent of
his unlimited propensity for reckless japing — but
never so much as now. 'I was a fool — but — but—
thank goodness you fellows stopped me. But — Tal-

bot's told us that the notes have been found hidden in his desk. Who hid them there?'

Neither Tom Merry nor Manners answered that. By whose hand but the Toff's could it have been done?

CHAPTER XXVIII

A RIFT IN THE LUTE

'BAI Jove!' murmured Arthur Augustus D'Arcy.
  He looked concerned.

It was the following day. After third school
Arthur Augustus was sauntering in the quad with
his accustomed elegance and grace. The sight of
the Terrible Three caused him to frown slightly,
with a recollection of the trousers that had been
ruined in No. 10 study when he had sat in the inky
gum in the arm-chair. But a moment or two later
he forgot those trousers as Talbot of the Shell came
along.

Talbot was walking with his eyes on the ground,
as if in deep thought. But as he glanced up and saw
the other Shell fellows he coloured, changed his
direction, and walked away more quickly.

Tom Merry and Manners and Lowther stood
looking after him as he went. And Arthur Augustus
murmured 'Bai Jove!' and looked concerned.

Generally Talbot was on the best of terms with
the Three. Now, obviously, he was deliberately

avoiding them. Plainly there was a rift in the lute.

Tom Merry looked uncomfortable. Manners shrugged his shoulders. Monty Lowther flushed. They made no move to follow Talbot.

'Bai Jove!' repeated Arthur Augustus. And he bore down on the Terrible Three.

'Cheeky ass!' Lowther was muttering.

'He's got his back up!' said Tom Merry, with a clouded brow.

'No wonder — if he thinks —!' said Manners slowly.

The dulcet tones of Arthur Augustus D'Arcy interrupted.

'You fellows been wowin'?' he asked.

'No, ass!' said Tom.

'Weally, Tom Mewwy —'

'Run away and play, kid,' said Lowther.

'Weally, Lowthah —'

'Br-r-r-r!' grunted Monty.

'I do not wegard that as an intelligent wemark, Lowthah. If you fellows have been wowin' with old Talbot pewwaps I could set it wight,' suggested Arthur Augustus encouragingly. 'You can wely on a fellow of tact and judgement, you know. What's the trouble?'

The Shell fellows were not likely to tell Arthur Augustus what the trouble was. So far nothing had

been said of the discovery in Talbot's study —
Railton, for some reason the juniors could not
fathom, had been silent on the subject. Talbot had
fully expected to be taken before the Head: but
it had not happened. Why the house-master had
taken no steps in the matter was a mystery to Talbot,
and to the Three, since he had told them of the
discovery. But Railton had taken none so far as
they knew.

Arthur Augustus gazed inquiringly at them. But
he received no answer to his question.

'Pway cough it up, deah boys,' he said. 'When
fwiends fall out what is needed is a spot of tact and
judgement fwom a mutual fwiend. Pway confide
in me what is the mattah.'

Still no reply.

'Pway wegard me as a peacemaker,' urged Arthur
Augustus.

'Fathead!' said Manners.

'Weally, Mannahs —'

'Oh, I'll tell him,' said Monty Lowther. Even
in the troubling and painful circumstances, Monty
could not help being funny, 'If you'll keep it dark,
Gussy —'

'Yaas, wathah.'

'Not a word to a single soul!' said Lowther, im-
pressively.

'Not a syllable, deah boy.'

'Then I'll tell you.'

'Look here, Monty —!' exclaimed Manners.

'Pway do not intewwupt, Mannahs,' said Arthur Augustus. 'Go on, Lowthah. What have you got against old Talbot?'

'You're sure you won't tell a soul?'

'Yaas, wathah.'

'Honour bright?'

'Honah bwight, deah boy. What is it?'

'We don't like the way he does his back hair!' said Monty Lowther, gravely.

'Wha-a-t?' ejaculated Arthur Augustus blankly.

'Mind you keep it dark!' added Lowther. 'Tell it not in Gath, whisper it not in the streets of Askalon —'

Tom Merry and Manners chuckled. The expression on Arthur Augustus's noble countenance was quite entertaining.

'You uttah ass!' exclaimed Arthur Augustus. 'Lowthah, I wegard you as a funnay fathead! If you mean that you will not tell me what is the mattah —'

'What a brain!' said Lowther. 'He's guessed it.'

'Weally, Lowthah —'

The Terrible Three, grinning, walked on: leaving Arthur Augustus frowning. But his frown faded out. Arthur Augustus was a kind-hearted fellow, and he was quite concerned about a spot of trouble between friends. He was going to set it right if he could.

As he had derived no information from the Terrible Three he ambled away after Talbot. The latter was about to go into the House when Gussy overtook him and tapped him on the arm.

'Talbot, deah boy —!' began Arthur Augustus.

The Shell fellow looked round impatiently.

'Well, what?' he asked.

'I twust you will not wegard me as buttin' in, Talbot,' said Arthur Augustus with dignity, 'But I could not help noticin' that you are not on the usual fwiendly terms with Tom Mewwy and Mannahs and Lowthah —'

Talbot compressed his lips.

'Well?' he almost snapped.

'I am vewy sowwy to see it, and I think pewwaps I could set the mattah wight,' explained Arthur Augustus. 'Pwobably it is only some twifle which a fellow of tact and judgement could cleah up quite easily. Pewwaps you will tell me what the twouble is, deah boy.'

Talbot gave him a look and, without replying, turned and walked into the House. Arthur Augustus fairly blinked after him.

'Bai Jove!' he ejaculated.

Evidently there was no information to be derived from Talbot of the Shell. Once more it was borne in upon Gussy's mind that Talbot's manners were deteriorating! He shook his noble head sadly. There was a deep frown on his brow when Blake and Herries and Digby joined him, and they looked at him inquiringly.

'What's up?' asked Herries.

'Anything come between the wind and your nobility, old bean?' asked Blake.

'I wegard that as a widiculous question, Blake. There is some twouble on between No. 10 study and Talbot, and I should be vewy glad to set it wight, but I could not get anythin' out of those thwee but an idiotic joke from Lowthah, and when I asked Talbot he actually walked away without answerin'. His mannahs are weally becomin' deplorable. I do not see anythin' furthah that I can do in the mattah,' added Arthur Augustus with dignity. 'If they want to wow, they can wow, and I shall let them wip!'

CHAPTER XXIX

IN SUSPENSE

TALBOT tapped at the door of Mr. Railton's study, and entered.

His face was set.

The house-master, at his study table, looked across it at the Shell fellow. It was not the usual kindly glance he had always had for Talbot. His face was stern, his look icy.

'Mr. Railton —!' began Talbot.

The house-master interrupted him.

'Why have you come here? I did not send for you.'

'I have been expecting to be sent for,' said Talbot, bitterly. 'I had expected to have seen Dr. Holmes before this, and to have been sent away from this school in disgrace.'

'Well?'

'What does this mean?' exclaimed Talbot. 'I have a right to know. You do not believe that I know nothing of the notes you found in my desk yesterday —'

The house-master's lip curled.

'Do you expect me to believe any such thing?' he rapped.

'No!' said Talbot, in a low voice. 'I cannot expect you to believe anything of the kind, sir. It is asking too much. It is true — but you cannot believe it — in your place I know that I could not believe it. But if you believe me to be what you suppose, why this delay? Why am I kept in suspense? Even if you believe me guilty you have no right to play cat-and-mouse. This in unendurable. Take me to Dr. Holmes and let there be an end.'

The house-master sat silent, looking at him. In spite of what seemed irrefragable, incontrovertible evidence, something of his old faith in the boy still lingered. His stern face was troubled.

Talbot broke the silence.

'I must ask you a question, sir!' he said. 'Something has happened that may perhaps change your belief.'

'I should be glad to hear it,' said Mr. Railton dryly.

'One day you lost the key to your money-drawer. It was picked up by a junior of this House two or three weeks ago —'

'That is so,' said Mr. Railton, staring at him. 'It

was found by Lowther, and Merry brought it back to me.'

'What happened once might happen again,' said Talbot. 'If the key were lost a second time it may have been found — and used.'

'The key was not lost a second time,' said Mr. Railton, in the same dry tone. 'I found that there was a slit in the lining of my pocket, through which the key must have slipped the day it was dropped on the stairs. The key has been kept safely since.'

Talbot breathed hard.

'I have a right to ask you, sir,' he said. 'Can you say with absolute certainty that that key has been safely in your keeping since? That it was safely in your keeping when your money-drawer was opened the night before last?'

'I can say so with absolute certainty,' answered Mr. Railton. 'The key has been on my own person ever since Tom Merry handed it back to me.'

Talbot stood silent.

His last faint hope died away.

In such a matter, he knew, Railton would not speak without absolute certainty. The key had not been lost a second time. His suspicion of Monty Lowther was unfounded. It had seemed to let in a ray of light where all was dark: but there was nothing in it. He had clung to the thought, to the

hope, that this affair might turn out to be nothing
but an insensate practical joke. That thought faded
from his mind now, and that hope from his heart.

'Nothing of the kind occurred, or could have
occurred!' said Mr. Railton. 'My key was not used
to open that drawer on Tuesday night. The lock
was picked by a skilful and cunning cracksman.
The purloined notes were found hidden in your
study — the currency notes. The bank-notes are
still missing. If you have come here to confess
where they are —'

'I know no more than you do, sir.'

Mr. Railton made an impatient gesture.

'You may leave my study,' he said.

'I must speak, sir! If I am judged guilty, if my
head-master decides as you have already decided,
I must go. It is not fair to me to keep me in this
suspense. Let there be an end.'

Mr. Railton nodded slowly.

'I acknowledge that, Talbot,' he said. 'Of my
own will I should have taken you to Dr. Holmes
yesterday after the discovery I made in your
study. But I am not wholly my own master in
this matter.'

'I don't understand —'

'I placed the affair in the hands of Inspector
Skeat,' said Mr. Railton. 'I am bound to act as he

advises, having done so — in fact, I have given him my word to that effect.'

Talbot stared.

'Is it Inspector Skeat, then, who is playing cat-and-mouse with me?' he exclaimed.

'Kindly do not use such expressions, Talbot! Mr. Skeat is an experienced police-officer, and he must have his reasons, though I admit that I do not know what they are. But he made it a point, upon which he insisted, that nothing should be said in public of this affair until he gave the word. Having promised to carry out his instructions I cannot depart from them. I reported the discovery to him, as you may guess, and he repeated that it was important, indeed urgent, that nothing should be said of the matter.'

'I cannot understand why —'

'Neither can I,' said Mr. Railton. 'But I must trust to the Inspector's judgement. I have explained this, Talbot, so that you may know that it is not by my wish that you remain in suspense. Until Inspector Skeat gives me leave to take action nothing will be said, and nothing will be done.'

'And all the while —!' muttered Talbot, 'All the while, I'm to mix with the other fellows and go on as if nothing had happened — all the while —' He broke off, with a sudden exclamation, and his eyes gleamed. 'Inspector Skeat can have only one motive for this, sir — only one.'

'Indeed!' said Mr. Railton, 'and what may that be, Talbot, if you know more than I do.'

'He doubts my guilt,' said Talbot.

The house-master started.

'That can be his only reason, sir! That must be it! He is not so sure as you are, sir, that I am the ungrateful reptile you believe me to be!' said Talbot, bitterly. 'There is at least a doubt in his mind — it must be so.'

'I shall hope that you are right, Talbot!' said the house-master slowly. 'Heaven knows how gladly I would see you cleared of this dreadful charge. But matters must remain as they are until I hear from Inspector Skeat. Now leave my study.'

Talbot left the study without speaking again. He was to remain in suspense — not knowing from one day to another, from one hour to another, when he was to be called before his head-master. But if there was a doubt in the mind of Inspector Skeat it was at least a gleam of light — a glimmer of hope.

He almost ran into the Terrible Three as he came out of the House. Tom Merry caught him by the arm and stopped him.

'Look here, Talbot, old man —' he began.

'Look here—!' said Manners, at the same moment.

'Look here —!' said Monty Lowther, like an echo.
Talbot smiled faintly.

'I'm sorry, Lowther,' he said. 'I-I ought to have
taken your word. I know now that it was not one of
your mad japes — You couldn't have had the key—
I know that from Railton. But-but — well, I'm
sorry! Now you'd better leave me alone.'

'Hold on,' said Tom.

'Don't be a goat, Tom! Listen to this — any hour,
any minute, I may be called up before the Head and
sacked — even if it's no worse — and it may be!
Keep clear of me in time.'

He dragged at his arm. But Tom held on to it,
and Manners took the other arm, and held on to
that. Talbot looked from face to face.

'I tell you —!' he muttered.

'You can tell us anything you like,' said Tom,
steadily, 'but we're sticking to you, old man! We
can't understand what's happened any more than
you can — but we know you're straight as a die,
and we're sticking to you, through thick and thin!
And that's that!'

'That's precisely and exactly that!' said Manners.

'Just that!' said Monty Lowther.

'But —!' stammered Talbot.

'But us no buts!' said Lowther, 'Argue us no
arguments and jaw us no jaw! We're sticking to

you whether you like it or not. Now put a sock in it.'

And Talbot said no more. His heart was lighter as he went into the quad with his friends. When the crash came — and it had to come soon — at least he had three faithful friends to stand by him, through thick and thin.

CHAPTER XXX

CALLED TO HEEL

SKIMPOLE came into No. 9 study and blinked through his glasses at the junior who sat by the window, with a volume of Livy in his hands.

Titus Livius was not an author to whom many St. Jim's fellows cared to devote their leisure hours. But Talbot was a studious fellow, and he found relief from harassing thoughts in study.

'Oh, there you are, Talbot,' bleated Skimpole.

Talbot looked up from the Carthaginian War.

'Here I am, Skimmy,' he answered. 'Want anything?'

Poor Skimmy, with his scientific predilections, was something of a butt in his form, but Talbot was always kind and considerate to him, and the trouble on his mind did not make him less so. If Skimmy wanted help with a French exercise or a Latin translation, even if he wanted to babble about the 'Gaseous Origin of Mind and Matter', Talbot was prepared to be patient and obliging. But on the present occasion it was none of these things that had brought Skimpole up to No. 9.

'I have a note for you, Talbot,' he explained.

'A note?' repeated Talbot in surprise.

'Yes! I was out of gates,' Skimpole further explained, 'And a man asked me to take in a note to you. I did not like his looks very much, Talbot, but as he said that it was important I thought I would do as he asked.'

Skimpole groped in a pocket and produced an envelope. Talbot, in surprise, held out his hand for it. Why any person out of gates should have sent in a note for him he could not guess.

He slit the rather grubby envelope and drew out a folded sheet of grubby paper. He unfolded the paper and looked at it.

Then he gave a violent start.

'Smug!' he breathed.

His brows contracted, and a glitter came into his eyes.

He had almost forgotten the existence of Smug Purkiss. The man had gone — the drastic lesson he had received had been enough for him. Talbot had never expected to hear from him again. He was prepared, more than prepared, to repeat the lesson if Smug asked for it. But he had never expected Smug to ask. And this was from Smug! It ran:

Dear Toff,

   I got to see you. No hard feelings, Toff. You'll find
me a friend. Come to the same place, and make it
five o'clock if you can. I'll wait anyway. If I don't
see you I'll walk on to the school.

                                                          Smug

   Talbot crumpled the note in his clenched hand.
His eyes were blazing. There was a threat in that
brief missive: Smug's lesson, after all, had not been
enough for him. It was a threat and order! He knew
that Talbot would come rather than let him 'walk
on to the school'.
   'The rat,' breathed Talbot.
   Skimpole blinked at him.
   'Is anything the matter, Talbot?' he asked.
   'Oh! Yes — no — no —!' stammered Talbot. He
had forgotten Skimmy for the moment.
   'I hope I was right to bring in the note!' said
Skimmy, anxiously. 'I did not like the man's looks
much, but —'
   'Oh! Yes, yes, quite right,' said Talbot. 'Thanks,
Skimmy. Quite all right, old chap!' He thrust the
note into his pocket and rose.
   Skimpole picked up 'The Gaseous Origin of
Mind and Matter' and sat down to it. Talbot hastily
left the study.

'This way, old fellow,' called out Tom Merry from the doorway of No. 10. 'Tea in this study.'

Talbot glanced round at him.

'Thanks, Tom — not now! I've got something I must do,' and he hurried down the passage before Tom could reply.

On the study landing he paused. He had to think. Smug would be waiting at the 'same place'; the old hut in Wayland Wood. If Talbot did not go he would come on to the school — a visit from an old acquaintance of the Angel Alley gang at a time when the 'Toff' was already under suspicion! Talbot clenched his hands almost convulsively. Yet he was puzzled, for what did the man want? He had been knocked out, as a warning: and he was asking for the same again! He was going to get it — hard! But why? What purpose did the man hope to serve by forcing him to another meeting?

He could not guess.

'The rat!' breathed Talbot again. 'I must go — he knows that! But he shall repent it! If it came out that I had seen him — if anyone knew — and and Skeat must know —'

He remembered his promise to Inspector Skeat. Somehow, he could not begin to guess how, the Inspector had foreseen that Smug might communicate with him again. He had asked to be in-

formed immediately if it occurred — and now it
had occurred. He had to let the Inspector know.

He descended the stairs at last.

It was easy to obtain permission from Master
Linton, his form-master, to make a call on his
telephone. Talbot found the master of the Shell
in Common-Room, and Linton gave leave at once.
Certainly he never dreamed that it was to the
police station at Wayland that that call was to
be made.

Talbot hurried to Mr. Linton's study, hurried
in and closed the door after him. A moment more
and he was dialling the police station. A voice came
through in reply.

'Wayland 101.'

'Can I speak to Inspector Skeat — ?'

'Who's speaking?'

'Tell him Talbot, from the School.'

'Hold on.'

There was a pause: and then the rather fruity
voice of Inspector Skeat came through.

'Is that Master Talbot?'

'Talbot speaking. You asked me to let you know
if I heard anything from Smug Purkiss again,'
breathed Talbot.

'And you have heard?' There was an alert note
in the fruity voice.

'Yes: he has had the impudence to send in a note to me by another fellow. That's why I've rung you up, Mr. Skeat. I promised to let you know.'

'I am glad you have kept that promise, Master Talbot.'

'Even the "Toff" does not forget a promise, Mr. Skeat,' said Talbot bitterly. 'I cannot see what use it is, as you have told me that there is no charge against the rogue at present: but I have done what you asked me to do. That is all.'

'One moment, Master Talbot. What is in the note?'

'Only what he asked me before on the phone. I am to meet him again — or he will come to the school.'

'And you are going?'

'I must.'

'With what intention?'

Talbot gritted his teeth.

'To make him sorry that he has dared to give me orders, Mr. Skeat. To make him understand that he had better keep clear of me.'

'Where is the meeting?'

'What does that matter?'

'I have asked you a question, Master Talbot. Please answer it.'

'At the old hut, near the footpath in Wayland

Wood — where I met him before — you know the place as well as I do —'

'Quite! And when?'

'At five o'clock today.'

'Very good, Master Talbot. I have taken note of what you have told me. Good-bye!' And Inspector Skeat rang off.

Talbot jammed the receiver back on the hooks, and left Mr. Linton's study. Why Mr. Skeat was interested in that meeting he did not know: and he cared little. His thoughts concentrated on Smug. The man he had warned off had come back — and he should be sorry that he had come!

He glanced up at the clock-tower as he came out of the House. It was not yet time to start for the rendezvous. But Talbot did not go up to Tom Merry's study. He was in no mood for the company of even his best friends. He had been called to order by Smug Purkiss — called to heel like a dog! Already under suspicion, condemned by his housemaster, waiting in suspense for the final blow, this was added! His face was set, his eyes glinting under knitted brows, when at length he went out of gates and started to walk to the old hut in Wayland Wood.

CHAPTER XXXI

DOWN AND OUT

SMUG PURKISS lounged along the shady footpath in Wayland Wodd, his hands in his pockets,
a cigarette in his mouth. He stopped about half-
way through the wood and stood leaning on a
tree-trunk, lighting a fresh cigarette. As he smoked
it he stared along the footpath in the direction of
Rylcombe Lane: which was the direction by which
anyone would come from St. Jim's. It was nearly
five o'clock: and at any moment he expected to see
a sturdy, well-set-up figure on the path: for he had
no doubt that Talbot would come. And at length,
in the distance, he had a glimpse of a schoolboy's
cap with a red stripe, and he knew that Talbot was
coming.

Smug grinned.

He detached himself from the tree, and plunged
into the thickets behind it. Thick underwoods grew
round the old abandoned hut: branches and twigs
rustled as Smug pushed his way through. He
reached the old hut and tramped in, his foxy eyes

glancing round him as he entered. All was silent
and deserted in that solitary spot: there was no sign
that any foot had trodden there since Smug's last
meeting with Talbot of the Shell. Smug gave a nod
of satisfaction, threw away the stump of his cigarette
through a gap in the old crumbling wall, and lighted
another. Then his hand slid into his pocket and
came out again with something in it — and that
something was a sock wrapped round a length of
leaden pipe. At the last meeting Smug had been
knocked right and left, and had remained groaning
on the earth when Talbot had done with him. This
time Smug had come prepared for trouble. With
that deadly 'cosh' in his hand he did not fear the
schoolboy's fists. The 'cosh' supplied the place of
the courage he lacked.

He waited.

It was some little time before a rustling in the
thickets anounced that Talbot was at hand. He
was coming — but he came slowly. Smug gave
a low chuckle. He could guess the schoolboy's
reluctance to meet him — to see or hear anything
of him. But Talbot, though he came slowly,
came — and at length he stepped into the dim
old hut.

Smug have him a nod.

'I figured you'd come, "Toff"!' he said. The

boy's look of scorn and loathing brought only a grin to his hard, foxy face.

'You knew I would come!' said Talbot quietly. 'It was that or seeing you at my school: and more than ever now I do not want that. But I think you will be sorry that you made me come.'

'Guess again!' said Smug. He half-drew the cosh from his pocket. 'See that? I've cracked 'eads with that, "Toff" — more'n once. And I'd crack yours as soon as look at you. Last time we was here you knocked me out — I could 'ardly crawl away after you was through. But you ain't handling a covey this time, "Toff". You lift a 'and and you get it, 'ard.'

He was watchful as a cat, keeping the cosh in his hand.

Talbot's lip curled with contempt.

'You a man — and I a boy!' he said, 'And you come armed. You crawling reptile —'

'No 'ard words, "Toff", and no 'ard feelings,' said Smug. 'I've just warned you not to come the rough stuff, that's all. We're 'ere for a talk, and you're going to 'ear of something to your advantage, like they say in the advertisements. I'm your friend, if you look at it the right way — and I'll say that you want a friend, the way things has been going up at your school. What?' he chuckled.

Talbot gave a violent start.

'What do you mean — how can you know any-thing about what has happened at the school?' he panted.

Smug chuckled again.

'You'd be surprised!' he grinned. 'I reckon I know as much as you could tell me, "Toff". Ain't there been a robbery at your school?'

Talbot stared blankly. Never had he been so utterly taken by surprise.

'How could you know?' he exclaimed. 'How could you have spied that out? Nothing has been said — it is not even known in the school — only to two or three — yet you —'

'I know more'n that!' grinned Smug. 'Ain't a lock been picked that only the "Toff" could pick: and ain't your schoolmaster had sense enough to know that you did it because nobody else could?'

Talbot stood dumb, staring.

The man knew: how, was beyond his fathoming.

'Spill it, "Toff"!' grinned Smug. 'Ain't I got it right?'

'Yes,' breathed Talbot.

'Ain't it put on you?'

'Yes,' the boy breathed again.

'Ain't they searched for the missing money?'

'Yes.'

'And ain't they found it in your desk?'

'Yes.'

'Jest as I figured!' said Smug, with a nod. 'All that beats me is that you're still at the school and ain't been hoofed out yet. That's what I expected to foller at once, but it ain't follered yet. But I guess it's coming, "Toff", ain't it?'

'Yes,' Talbot muttered again, 'it's coming.'

'I banked on it!' grinned Smug.

Talbot made a step nearer. Smug gripped his cosh. But the schoolboy did not raise a hand. He only stared intently into the evil, foxy face.

'You know the whole story!' said Talbot. His voice was quiet. 'There is only one way you could know, Purkiss. You —!' He paused, watching the man's face.

'Guessed it?' sneered Smug.

The grin faded from his face. His foxy eyes gleamed at Talbot: all the evil in the man's nature was in the look he gave the schoolboy.

'You figured that I was gone,' he said, between his teeth. 'You beat me — beat me like a dog — you turned me down, and beat me: and you fancied that I'd gone and forgotten it all! Not 'alf, "Toff"! I'd have got level if the darbies was going to be clapped on me the next minute. I'd have laid for you with a cosh in my 'and if there 'adn't been a better way.'

'A better way!' breathed Talbot.

'You 'eld your 'ead 'igh,' jeered Smug. 'You, that was the "Toff", the boy cracksman of Angel Alley — you 'eld your 'ead 'igh, you did — you wouldn't touch the likes of me, 'cept with your knuckles, cuss you. But I've brought you down from your perch, "Toff" — I've brought you right down into the mire and the mud — I've brought you down so that you'll 'ave to go back to the old game, 'cause there'll be nothing else left — that's what you asked for, "Toff", when you knocked me out in this 'ere hut, and that's what's come to you.'

'You!' breathed Talbot. His brain seemed almost in a whirl. 'I don't understand how — how —!'

'Easy!' said Smug contemptuously. 'I knowed you was at the school, didn't I? You fancied I was gone.' He laughed savagely. 'I wasn't gone, "Toff" — I was lying low. Nearer than you fancied, "Toff" — sometimes. Think I couldn't open a winder without leaving a trace? I ain't the 'and with a safe that you always was, "Toff" — but I'm no slouch. Why, you booby, three or four nights I was in your school, getting my bearings afore I hit.'

'Oh!' breathed Talbot, 'The prowler —' He knew now. It was not some unknown, unthinking School House junior who had 'prowled' the House at night. It was this wary rascal getting his bearings. If, on the night when he had kept watch, he had caught the prowler, it was Smug Purkiss that he would have caught!

The grin came back to Smug's foxy face. The dumbfounded look on Talbot's seemed to amuse him.

'That was the how of it!' he went on gloatingly. 'I knew how to fix you, "Toff", and I fixed you okay. They never knowed they had a visitor o'nights when they was all asleep in their little bunks. I got my bearings, "Toff" — I looked out names in the books in the studies and found which was yours — easy, "Toff"! Child's play, "Toff"! I had your desk marked out to hide the notes — think I couldn't open it, "Toff", though I never had your 'and with a safe! I'd have put some in your box in your dormitory, too, only there I had bad luck. One night some young cub was awake and swiped me with a piller — another night, another young cub drenched me with ink — but they never saw me, "Toff" — they never knowed who it was they pillered and drenched. If I'd found you in your dormitory I'd have found your box soon enough — but arter that, "Toff", I chucked rootin' in the sleeping quarters — them young cubs seemed to wake up too easy.'

Talbot stood silent, loking at the man.

He knew it all now.

'But I found out as much as I wanted to know,' went on Smug. 'I found out where money was kept in a master's study: and when I got on to that it was all set for the final.' He chuckled. 'I figured out what would follow, because it had to foller, "Toff" — and from what you've said, it went like clockwork! Didn't it?'

'It did!' breathed Talbot.

'And now you're down and out!' said Smug, viciously. 'Now you've got what was coming to you, "Toff"!'

'Yes,' said Talbot quietly, 'You succeeded all along the line Smug — and I'm down and out. Why are you telling me?'

Smug laughed an unpleasant laugh.

'Two reasons!' he said. 'Fust, I wanted you to know that I got level with you for 'andling me. It ain't enough to hit a covey, if he don't know who hit him. I'm rubbing that in, "Toff".'

'You would!' said Talbot, contemptuously. 'And what if I go to my house-master, or to the police station at Wayland and tell them all that you have let out?'

Smug laughed again.

'Tell your great-grandmother,' he jeered. 'Think I'd have put you wise if there was a dog's chance that anybody would believe a word of it if you

told them? You got sense, "Toff", 'igh and mighty
as you are — you know they'd think it the biggest
lie a crook ever told to squirm out of a scrape.'

Talbot was silent, thinking.

He nodded at last.

'Yes,' he said, 'such a story would sound much
too steep — told by the "Toff", already found
guilty. Yes!'

'You said it,' grinned Smug. 'I wanted you to
know, "Toff", but you'd never have knowed if it
would do me any 'arm.'

'I understand that! And what was your other
reason — you said you had two?' said Talbot
quietly.

'I want your 'elp, "Toff".'

'My help?' repeated Talbot.

'You ain't forgotten the proposition I put up
last time we was 'ere,' said Smug, 'You cut up
rusty — you knocked me out. I've paid you back
for that — paid you up in full, ain't I?'

'You have!' said Talbot.

'I got level,' said Smug, 'and now you're back
where you was, "Toff" — and when you're kicked
out of your school it's the old game for you. I've
got level, "Toff" — and I've got you where I want
you. Come in with me on the Wayland Grange
lay, "Toff" — that's your best guess.'

Talbot stood breathing hard.

He understood it all now. It was for revenge
that the gangster had done what he had done: but
he had had another motive — he needed the
'Toff's' skill: and he still hoped to make use of
him. To his evil mind the outcome seemed
certain — the 'Toff', driven out in disgrace, would
turn back to the old life — to what else could he
turn? That he would have died sooner was a fact
that a mind like Smug's could never assimilate.
He had revenged himself upon the schoolboy who
had 'handled' him — and now he had the 'Toff'
where he wanted him. That was Smug's belief.
Now he was going to use him!

'It's a fortune, "Toff"!' he said. 'I tell you there's
thousands to be picked up at the Grange —'

'You villain!' muttered Talbot.

'No 'ard words, "Toff" —'

'Listen to me,' said Talbot. 'You've been too
cunning for me, Smug, and I'm down and
out. I've no defence — I shall be turned out
of my school — in such disgrace that I cannot
face my uncle, my only relative. I shall be
thrown on the world. I shall be an outcast. But
sooner than touch a penny that is not my own
I will perish on the roads. You have succeeded
in one way, Smug. But you have failed in

another — you cannot drag me down to your level.'

'Sez you!' sneered Smug. 'Look 'ere, "Toff", come off it! I've fixed you so's you got no other way. I've dished you at your school — that's shut against you from now on. You got to go back to what you was in Hookey Walker's gang. You got no choice now. I tell you I've fixed it for you to have no choice — and you've got to bite on it. Now what you going to do?'

Talbot looked at him steadily.

'I'll tell you!' he said. 'I'm going straight — whatever may happen. You couldn't understand it, and I expect you couldn't believe it — but that's that. And before we part, Smug, you're going to hand me the bank-notes to take back where they belong.'

'The bank-notes!' repeated Smug.

'Eighty pounds were taken from my house-master's desk,' said Talbot. 'Only the currency notes — thirty pounds — were found hidden in my study. The bank-notes have not been found.' His lip curled bitterly. 'The currency notes were enough to fix me — you kept the bank-notes and you have them now. You are going to hand them over to me. They are going back to Mr. Railton.'

'I don't think!' said Smug derisively. 'I played that game in your school, "Toff", to fix you — but

I wasn't coming away empty-'anded. Not likely. And that ain't all — when them notes is passed, "Toff", who do you think will get the blame? Not me, "Toff" — you!'

'I know that — now!' Talbot's voice was very quiet. 'And I know what I am going to do, you rat.'

'Come in with me, "Toff", and share —'

'That will do! I've heard enough from you, Smug! Will you hand over the bank-notes?'

'Not so's you'd notice it,' jeered Smug.

'Then I shall take them — and I shall give you what you've asked for,' said Talbot between his teeth.

Smug whipped out the cosh.

'Stand back!' he snarled. 'You lift a finger —'

Talbot came at him. The cosh did not daunt him. He dodged a savage blow, and his clenched fist came home full in the evil face.

Smug staggered, with a panting howl. Then, with cat-like fury he flung himself at the schoolboy, and the cosh whirled in the air.

Neither of them in the excitement of the moment noticed that a plump figure had suddenly appeared in the gap in the wall of the old hut. But as the cosh went up for a fierce crashing blow Smug's arm was suddenly grasped from behind and dragged back. The next moment the cosh was snatched from his hand.

Smug's arm was suddenly grasped from behind and dragged back

He whirled round in amazement and rage. Talbot uttered a cry of astonishment. He had believed that they were alone at the hut in the wood. The sudden sight of Inspector Skeat almost made him wonder whether he was dreaming. He stared blankly as the plump Inspector grasped the gangster, and Smug crumpled in that grasp.

There was a clink of metal.

Smug Purkiss, panting with rage, stood tottering, the handcuffs on his wrists. Inspector Skeat glanced at the astonished schoolboy and gave him a nod. Evidently Mr. Skeat had been in cover behind the old hut.

'You!' gasped Talbot.

'I,' the plump Inspector smiled. 'You did not expect to see me here, Master Talbot —'

'No! I never dreamed —'

'Neither did this precious rogue,' smiled the Inspector. 'Follow me, my lad.'

With a hand on his collar, the Inspector propelled the gangster out of the hut. Talbot stood staring after them blankly. It was some minutes before he left the hut and followed the Inspector and his prisoner up the footpath to Wayland.

CHAPTER XXXII

LIGHT AT LAST

'MERRY! What is it?'

Mr. Railton spoke sharply.

He was standing by the window of his study, looking out into the quadrangle with a frowning, thoughtful brow, when Tom Merry tapped at his door and entered. His frown did not relax as he turned his head. He was in a mood of painful and troubled thought, and for once his kind temper seemed to fail him.

He was thinking of Talbot — of the boy whose life had been so strange and chequered before he came to the school: but whom, until now, he would have trusted as he trusted Tom Merry of the Shell, or D'Arcy of the Fourth.

He could not but believe that Talbot had failed in that trust: and it was a heavy blow to him. But that was not all. It was not fair to the boy to keep him in suspense, whatever he was: if he had to go, as go he must, why the delay? It was Inspector Skeat who had insisted upon silence and inaction:

and the house-master could see no reason for it.

Now, from the window, he had glimpsed a portly figure in the falling dusk in the quadrangle. It was Inspector Skeat: and it seemed to the house-master that his plump, ruddy face had an expression of plump satisfaction on it: the look of a man satisfied with himself and things generally. That was far from being Mr. Railton's own mood.

It was not a happy moment for a junior to interrupt his troubled thoughts, Tom Merry realised that, as his house-master almost snapped at him. But he had come there with something to say: and he was going to say it.

'If I may speak to you, sir —!' he began.

'Be brief.'

'It's about Talbot, sir.'

Mr. Railton started.

'Talbot! What do you mean, Merry?'

'He told us what you found in his study yesterday, sir —'

The house-master compressed his lips.

'He should not have done so,' he said curtly. 'The matter at present is not to be talked of. Least of all should I have expected Talbot to talk of it.'

'We're his friends, sir — Lowther and Manners and myself,' said Tom. 'He has no one else.'

'Well?' rapped the house-master. 'I have told

you to be brief, Merry. I expect Mr. Skeat every
moment. If you have anything more to say —'

'I've got to speak, sir,' said Tom resolutely.
'I know what you think, after what you found in
Talbot's study. I can't understand what it all means
any more than old Talbot can — but there's one
thing I do know, and that is that Talbot never
touched those notes, sir.'

'Merry!'

'I'm quite certain of that, sir,' said Tom, steadily.
'I trust Talbot as I trust myself, sir. I'd as soon think
that I did it as that he did it. I-I thought I ought to
tell you so, sir. I thought you ought to know that
there are fellows here who believe him and trust
him whatever things may look like. We are standing
by him through thick and thin: and I feel sure, sir,
that when everything is known he will be cleared.'

Mr. Railton stood looking at him.

Tom half expected angry words. But the house-
master did not look angry. His brow was clouded
with troubled thought.

'I-I know it's a cheek to come here and speak to
you like this, sir,' Tom Merry coloured, 'but-but
I had to tell you. Talbot's friends trust him, and-
and-and you, sir —' Tom paused.

'Well?'

'You trusted him once, sir — you always thought

well of him — can't you trust him a little further, as we do?'

'That will do, Merry! You may leave my study.'

Tom Merry, in silence, turned to the door. But the doorway was almost blocked by a plump, portly figure that had arrived there.

Inspector Skeat bestowed a nod and a smile on the Shell fellow.

'Come in, come in, Mr. Skeat!' said the house-master. 'You may go, Merry.'

'Yes, sir!'

Inspector Skeat held up a plump hand.

'One moment, sir,' he said. 'Let Merry remain for a few minutes.'

Tom, about to pass out at the doorway, stopped. He looked at Mr. Skeat and he looked at Mr. Railton, hesitating.

'For what reason, Mr. Skeat?' Railton's voice was impatient.

'I have something to tell you, sir, that Merry had better hear,' said the Inspector. He smiled a plump smile. 'I had a talk with Master Merry yesterday, sir, when he affirmed his faith in his friend, and I think he should hear the good news —'

Tom gave a start.

'Good news!' he breathed.

'The best!' smiled Mr. Skeat.

Mr. Railton broke in.

'Skeat! If you will explain yourself —'

'I will do so without delay, sir! As you know, I kept an open mind in this somewhat peculiar case: waiting for further developments to shed light on it — and I have now to report to you, sir, that the matter is wholly cleared up — and that Talbot comes through without a stain on his character, sir.'

Mr. Railton almost staggered in his surprise.

Tom Merry gasped.

Inspector Skeat smiled: a plump, benevolent smile. Perhaps he was inwardly enjoying the effect his unexpected announcement had caused. For a moment or two there was dead silence in the study.

'Skeat,' Railton spoke at last. 'Is it possible — ?'

'Not only possible but a fact, sir.'

'Talbot — innocent —'

'Quite.'

'I-I hardly understand — the notes were found in his desk —'

'Planted there, sir, to be found.'

'Impossible! No one at this school —'

'It was no one at this school who was guilty, Mr. Railton. It was a person of whom, probably, you have never heard — but of whom I have heard a good deal,' said Mr. Skeat. 'That person, sir,

planted the currency notes in Talbot's desk, partly
to pay off a grudge, partly in order to disgrace the
boy and drive him back to old forgotten ways —
having a use for him, sir, if he succeeded — but
the bank-notes he kept for his own benefit —
and they were found on him, sir, when he was
searched at Wayland police station. You may take
it from me, sir, that the boy Talbot was innocent
throughout —'

'Oh!' gasped Mr. Railton.

His face had lighted up almost as brightly as Tom
Merry's. How the stolid, ruddy police-inspector had
discovered all this he did not know: but it was good
news to him — the best of good news.

'The guilty party, sir, is now in a cell at Wayland,' resumed Mr. Skeat. 'He will be duly dealt
with by the law, sir. And,' added Mr. Skeat, almost
grinning, 'I am sure you will not regret now, sir,
that I requested you to keep the matter private, now
that it transpires that Talbot is an innocent party—
as I half believed, and wholly hoped, all the while,
sir. It is as well that he was never accused, sir.'

He gave Tom Merry a cheery nod.

'Now you may go, Merry,' he said.

'Oh, sir!' gasped Tom. 'Thanks, and thanks a
thousand times — by gum I've got to see old Talbot —' He ran out of the study.

Inspector Skeat sat down and proceeded to explain the whole strange story — the house-master listening almost like a man in a dream. Tom Merry went down the corridor like a fellow walking on air.

CHAPTER XXXIII

NO GUM FOR GUSSY

ARTHUR AUGUSTUS D'ARCY jumped.

He was startled.

He was also alarmed.

His eyeglass dropped to the end of its cord and he stood, in No. 10 study, staring at the door.

Outside that door there were footsteps that stopped.

'Bai Jove!' breathed Arthur Augustus.

It had happened before! Now it had happened again! Arthur Augustus, in his new career as a bold, bad ragger, seemed to have absolutely no luck. Quite recently the Terrible Three had caught him in their study, with disastrous and ruinous results to his trousers. Now it looked as if they were going to catch him again!

Yet he had been very cautious. He had had an eye, and an eyeglass, on the three. He had seen Tom Merry go to Railton's study. He had seen Manners and Lowther in the quad, with their eyes on Inspector Skeat, as if interested in seeing him arrive at St. Jim's again. It had seemed a perfectly propitious moment for a visit to No. 10 study. This time, Gussy felt assured, he was not going to be cornered by the proprietors of that study: this time his elegant bags were in no danger. This time he was going to 'rag' that study with impunity, as a warning to Monty Lowther to keep his japing propensities within bounds, and to his friends to see that he did so. All was set fair — when those footsteps came up the passage and stopped at the door.

Arthur Augustus made a step towards that door — but paused. Last time he had parked himself behind the door, but there had been no escape. He changed direction and made a jump to the corner of the study where the arm-chair stood, backed out of the way. Gussy had a bottle of gum in his hand. He could guess how it would be used if the Terrible Three caught him there. Half of it had been used already: half remained in the bottle. Gussy trembled for his trousers! He shot behind the arm-chair with almost supersonic speed, and ducked low out of sight.

The door opened the next moment.

But Arthur Augustus was already deep in cover. He could not see who came into the study though he could hear that there were two of them. Neither could they see him. No one, naturally, could see

through the high, solid back of an arm-chair. But
their voices told him who they were.

'Old Skeat here again!' That was Monty Lowther's voice.

'Still at it!' grunted Manners.

'Know where Talbot is?'

'He went out of gates —'

'I-I wonder if old Skeat wants to see him —'

'I wonder.'

That was so much Greek to Arthur Augustus. He
could imagine no reason why 'old Skeat' should
want to see Talbot of the Shell!

'Who's been here?' exclaimed Lowther, suddenly.

'What — ?'

'Some ass has been spilling gum on the chairs —'

'Oh, my hat! Has that ass D'Arcy been playing
the giddy goat again? The silly ass —!'

'The dithering dummy!'

'Your fault, Monty. You put gum in his topper —'

'Bother his topper, and bother him! I wish we'd
come up sooner and caught him! I'd give him gum!'

Arthur Augustus, in the corner behind the arm-
chair, grinned breathlessly. So far, at least, the two
Shell fellows had no suspicion that the ragger was
still in the study. He heard a sound of rubbing and
brushing: Monty Lowther had taken a duster to the
gum. Behind the arm-chair Arthur Augustus was

as still and silent as a mouse with two cats at hand!

Again there were footsteps in the passage.

'Oh, here comes Tom — not much luck with Railton, I expect,' said Manners. 'Oh, it's Talbot.'

Talbot of the Shell came hurriedly into No. 10.

'Where's Tom?' he exclaimed.

'Gone to speak to Railton — may be up any minute,' answered Manners. 'What on earth's happened, Talbot?'

He stared at Talbot. Monty Lowther ceased to rub gum and stared at him also. They stared in surprise. Only too well they knew how heavy his heart had been that day: and, quiet and reserved as he was, he had been unable to look his usual cheerful self. But there was a change now. It was a rather startling change. His face was bright, his eyes shining: he looked like a fellow who had not a care in the world. He laughed as he met their surprised gaze.

'I've got news,' he said.

'Looks as if it's good news, to judge by your chivvy!' said Monty Lowther. 'Lost a tanner and found a quid?'

Talbot laughed again. Evidently he was in high spirits.

'I'm on top of the world,' he explained.

'How come?'

'It's all right! I want Tom to hear — I wish he'd

come up. It's all right, now, you fellows — Skeat has got the man. I think he's here now — he was a little ahead of me — we didn't come in together—'

'You've seen old Skeat?' asked Manners, mystified.

'Yes!' Talbot chuckled. 'Loking at him you fellows wouldn't guess that he could beat Sherlock Holmes at his own game, would you?'

'Hardly,' said Manners.

'Not in your lifetime,' said Lowther.

'He kept an open mind,' said Talbot, laughing; 'But he worked it out — slow but sure! Good old Skeat! I tell you, it's all right — everything's cleared up, thanks to him — I believe he's with Railton now, telling him — Railton knows it all by this time — hallo, here comes Tom.'

Tom Merry came into the study like a whirlwind.

'Seen Talbot?' he gasped. 'Oh, here you are, old man!'

'Here I am,' said Talbot. 'Jolly good news, Tom —'

'I've just had it from Skeat,' said Tom. 'Lowther, old chap — Manners, old man — it's all right — right as rain — everything in the garden is lovely — but tell us all about it, Talbot, old boy — we know hardly a thing so far. Better shut the door, though — we don't want this all over the House.'

Tom banged the door shut.

'No,' said Talbot. 'Least said soonest mended. But I'll tell you fellows the whole story — Oh, great pip!'

He broke off, staring at the corner of the study. In that corner an elegant figure had suddenly risen into view behind the arm-chair, and an eyeglass gleamed at the astonished Shell fellows.

'Gussy!' exclaimed Tom Merry, blankly.

'D'Arcy!' ejaculated Manners.

'That ass —!' hooted Monty Lowther. 'Here all the time. I'll give him gum!'

'Weally, Lowthah —!'

'What on earth are you doing there, Gussy?' exclaimed Talbot.

'Pewwaps you fellows will allow me to explain,' said Arthur Augustus, with dignity. 'I came heah to wag this study as a warnin' to that ass, Lowthah, not to play potty twicks in mine —'

'You gummed the chairs!' hooted Lowther.

'Yaas, wathah, and I should have gummed lots of things, just like you gummed my toppah, if you fellows had not come in! If you wag in a fellow's study, Lowthah, you must expect to be wagged in weturn. I took covah when you fellows came in, as I knew vewy well you would wuin my twousahs again if you found me with the gum —'

'And why have you shown up now?' asked Tom.

'Weally, Tom Mewwy, that question hardly needs an answah. Fwom what you said, you fellows were about to discuss somethin' of a pwivate nature, and I twust that you do not wegard me as capable of playin' the part of an eavesdwoppah!' said Arthur Augustus, with tremendous dignity. 'In the circs, I had no wesource but to show up at once, befoah you started sayin' things that I could not have helped hearin'.'

'Good old Gussy!' said Talbot, with a chuckle.

'Weally, Talbot —'

'Good old ass!' said Tom Merry.

'Weally, Tom Mewwy —'

'Good old fathead!' said Manners.

'Weally, Mannahs —'

'Come out of that corner and have some of your own gum!' said Lowther.

'Weally, Lowthah —'

'No gum for Gussy,' said Tom Merry, laughing. 'Pax, old man!' He threw open the study door. 'Pass, friend, and all's well!'

Arthur Augustus emerged from the corner. The Shell fellows were laughing, but Gussy kept a wary eye on Monty Lowther as he edged towards the door. At the doorway he paused and turned his eyeglass on the four.

'Fwom what I could not help hearin', you fellows, it seems that there has been some sort of twouble on,' he said.

'Sort of!' said Talbot.

'And that it is all ovah now?'

'Over and done with!' smiled Talbot.

'And evewythin' is all wight again?'

'Right as rain.'

'I am vewy glad to hear it,' said Arthur Augustus benevolently, 'vewy glad indeed. Gwattahs, deah boys!'

And with that, Arthur Augustus walked away gracefully down the passage — glad that the trouble, whatever it had been, was over, and still gladder to escape ungummed! The door banged shut again, and there was a buzz of cheery voices in No. 10: and when the bell rang for roll, four fellows emerged from that study and marched down the passage arm-in-arm, barging other fellows whom they met, in sheer exuberance of spirits: Talbot of the Shell, and the loyal pals who had stood by him through thick and thin.